W9-BVW-928

Other books by Jane Louise Curry

The Bassumtyte Treasure
Shadow Dancers
The Great Flood Mystery
The Lotus Cup
Back in the Beforetime
TALES OF THE CALIFORNIA INDIANS

(Margaret K. McElderry Books)

Me, Myself and I

Me, Myself and I

A TALE OF TIME TRAVEL

Jane Louise Curry

Margaret K. McElderry Books
NEW YORK

For Mike and Mark,
with love.

Copyright © 1987 by Jane Louise Curry
All rights reserved. No part of this book may be reproduced or transmitted in any form or by any means, electronic or mechanical, including photocopying, recording, or by any information storage and retrieval system, without permission in writing from the Publisher.

Margaret K. McElderry Books
Macmillan Publishing Company
866 Third Avenue
New York, NY 10022
Collier Macmillan Canada, Inc.

Composition by Maryland Linotype Composition Company
Baltimore, Maryland
Printed and bound by Fairfield Graphics
Fairfield, Pennsylvania
Designed by Barbara A. Fitzsimmons

Printed in the United States of America
First Edition

1 3 5 7 9 11 13 15 17 19 20 18 16 14 12 10 8 6 4 2

Library of Congress Cataloging-in-Publication Data
Curry, Jane Louise.
Me, myself and I.
Summary: Sixteen-year-old J. J. uses his mentor's invention to go into the past to exorcise his unreturned love for a beautiful girl, and discovers a mystery involving another of the professor's inventions.
[1. Science fiction. 2. Mystery and detective stories] I. Title.
PZ7.C936Me 1987 [Fic] 87–2681
ISBN 0–689–50429–2

Me, Myself and I

Mutt's Prologue

You're not going to believe all this. You're going to think, This guy is a real Loony Tune. Maybe so, but if I don't unload the whole story on somebody *now*, this minute, I'll bust. So you're elected.

Don't misunderstand me. I *think* I've got my act together. Finally. I think. As soon as I woke up this morning, I put everything on tape just to make sure all the stuff I learned yesterday didn't evaporate the way dreams do—and when I played it back, *I* almost didn't believe me.

The problem is, where to start. Eight years ago at the Bay Area Science Fair? But back then—until yesterday, in fact—I didn't know what all had happened "before." So to speak. So maybe the best way to tell you about the whole weird, nutty mix-up is to start with J. J.'s part in it. Just the way J. J. would tell it.

J.J.'s Story

1

Tuesday morning—*was* that only yesterday?—the sun was still shining like mad, birds were singing their little throats raw, and I was walking around six inches off the ground. By midafternoon everything was bass-ackwards, down-side-up, and inside-out.

Up until The Fatal Tuesday I was (or so you could say if it wasn't such a moldy old cliché) happy as a clam. After all, wasn't I *the* J. J. Russell? John James Russell, inventor at the tender age of ten of the Hovercopter and six other Hovertoys, a freshman at the university at twelve, the Boy Wonder of the electrical engineering department's graduating class at fourteen and, after that, the only graduate student chosen as research assistant to Professor Nicholas Poplov, world authority on holography and a stack of other things? And on top of all that, wasn't I Apollonia Armbruster's boyfriend?

If you've ever seen Polly Armbruster, you know what I mean. As I remember it, exactly four years ago Tuesday, at her fourteenth-birthday party, I asked Polly to go to the movies with me and, wonder of wonders, she said, "Yes." Yes to *me*, the one the girls in my class called "John James Nerd." Polly's not only a little older than me (well, O.K., two years older, but I'd always been mature for my age), she was the prettiest girl in Locke Junior High. And she said, "Yes"! She almost had to peel me off her dining-room ceiling, I was so far up in the air. From then on we went to the movies every Saturday afternoon, and the world, as they say, was my oyster. As it turned out, it was more like my lemon. But how was I to know?

I had this date with Polly for lunch on Tuesday. It was her birthday, and I was taking her to the Gilded Shrimp, this fish place she likes downtown. We went, but the rest of the day didn't exactly work out according to plan. I ended up in a weirder fix than you could dream up if you were paid for it, and with my whole life nearly gummed up. And Jacko's. And Mutt's, too.

No. Hold it there. If you're going to believe any of this, I've got to start even before Tuesday lunch and ease into the whole thing. Step by step. Cool and collected. So here goes.

Tuesday, April 12. Actually, Tuesday was pretty weird from the start. Like, from one o'clock in the morning. After supper at home Monday night I came over here to Professor Poplov's labs to put in an hour or so at my computer terminal. The project we were working on—a totally new kind of holographic projector—was so great that nothing but Apollonia Anne Armbruster—or maybe food—could keep me away from work for long. Just imagine a 3-D movie of—well, say, of Polly—that you can *walk around and watch from the side or the back* if you want to. That's what we were working on. Once the process was perfected, it was going to be worth a lot of money. A *lot*. But that meant matching down to milliseconds and thousandths of an inch the images from twenty-four Poplov microprojectors. I was at least six months, maybe more, away from getting the bugs out of the computer program that would combine all those images into one three-dimensional figure. So far all we had was a moving 3-D blur that wasn't all that much better than a ghost out of some cheapo horror movie.

Anyhow, the number-crunching I was doing Monday night kept on working out so well that by the time I looked at the clock it was after eleven. The thought of biking all the way home in the pitch dark didn't exactly grab me. Besides, I had to be on campus first thing in the morning to take Professor Poplov to the airport, so I phoned home to tell Mom I was sacking out in the lab. I checked all the windows and security locks from Lab A, which is more an outer office than a working lab, back through Lab B, where I worked, to Lab C. C is the innermost and far the biggest of the three, a huge barn-like space broken up into work and storage areas, with a lot of far-out equipment—like our own $750,000 molecular beam epitaxy machine—scattered around the place. (If anybody ever asks you what molecular beam epitaxy is, just look wise and change the subject. It's not part of what happened, so I can't stop to explain.) Lab C has a lot of high, midair catwalks, too, because it once housed the first experimental model of the famous Galaxitron (known back then as the Humongous Hulk).

Anyhow, the john was off Lab B, so that lab was where I set up the folding cot, hung my sports jacket and tie over the back of a chair, and was asleep two minutes after I hit the lumpy pillow. (Sports jacket and *tie?*—I can see the look on your face, but if you'd hit college at age twelve, you'd have gone for green hair and hipboots if you thought they'd make you look Mature and Serious. Me, I had no imagination.)

The silent alarm—silent in the lab, that is—must have gone off in the campus patrol office a bit past one a.m., because at ten past the cops arrived with yowling sirens, squealing tires, and a flourish of screeching brakes. They didn't find any sign of whoever or whatever had triggered the alarm. All the windows and doors were still secure. But while I was out in front talking to Captain Timmons, this guy came past on his way back to his dorm from his girl's house, and told us a power company cherry picker had gone roaring past him on up the road at eighty or ninety miles an hour. The cops found it later, abandoned out by the freeway on-ramp, but at that point there wasn't any reason for me to put two and two together. Besides, the only two I was interested in putting together were Polly and me, at the best table at the Gilded Shrimp.

I went back to bed and thought about that while I dozed my way back to sleep. It was Polly's birthday, and I had this gold locket I'd bought her—a heart with a real diamond in it, and no dinky little chip, either. I'd shot the last of my quarterly royalty check from the company that made my Hovertoys on it. We'd had to settle for a fancy lunch instead of a fancy supper because her granny down in Gilroy was giving her a birthday dinner. But at least, since I would be picking Polly up on my way back from the airport in Professor Poplov's big old Volvo, I would have four wheels instead of two for a change. I fell asleep in the middle of worrying whether I'd have enough time to stop at home and change from the sports jacket to my new blazer before I went on to her dorm.

The first cloud in my sky drifted over the Student Union while I was halfway through my breakfast Danish. It popped into my head that I hadn't checked with the Gilded Shrimp to make sure they had fresh lobster tails on the menu. Polly always ordered lobster tails. It was no good telling myself she wouldn't mind if they weren't fresh. She would. Her mom called her Particular Poll when she turned up her nose at something, and she turned up her nose a lot. Not that I minded. Polly knew what she liked, and I liked that. After all, she liked me, didn't she?

Still, it was probably O.K. By Tuesday lunch they'd be sure to have fresh lobsters from the Monday catch. Even if they didn't, Friday- or Saturday-caught lobsters could be fresh. Restaurants kept them alive in a tub of water until the last minute, didn't they? I picked my Danish into little bits and ate them one by one. For Polly's birthday everything *had* to go O.K. Better than.

By the time I got myself together and pedaled out to Professor Poplov's house, I was still ten minutes early.

But he wasn't there. The Volvo was in the carport, but his bike was gone from its place by the back door. I had a key, so I let myself in. In the kitchen a half-eaten bowl of cornflakes and a cup of cold coffee stood on the dining-nook table. The Professor's carry-on suitcase was standing out by the front door, ready to go. But empty. Typical. Professor Poplov may be a world-class whiz at plasma physics and Fourier optics, but outside the lab he could use a nursemaid. I took the suitcase back to his bedroom and packed his good shoes, and some clean shirts and shorts and socks and other stuff I figured he'd need for five days in Switzerland. Then, after I'd hung his only good suit in a suit bag, I had to go to the study and root around in the drifts of papers on his desk and worktable until I found all the pages of the speech he was going to give to the International Conference on Unified Field Theory. I packed it in the suitcase, and when I went out to sling the bags in the back seat of the car, there the car keys were, in the ignition. I keep telling him not to *do* that, and most of the time he's pretty good about it. At least this time it meant I didn't have to lose another ten minutes rooting through the overflowing laundry basket and all the drawers and wastebaskets, looking for them.

I knew where the Professor was. The Poplov Labs, where else? He'd had an idea, and dropped everything to go work it out. Anybody else would have a computer terminal at home, or a computer and modem so he could log into the lab computer by phone. Not Professor Poplov. At work he used his own computer, never the university system's terminal, which is what I usually worked on. "If you do not have your lab computer on-line with the university mainframe computer, or plugged into the telephone system, no one can talk it into betraying your secrets," he said. Maybe he had a point, but he was such a nut on security, with his push-button combination locks and window-vibration alarms, that it was hard to take any of it seriously. You'd think we were working on some far-out military fairy tale like invisibility or force-field barriers instead of a little fancy holography. As for holograms—you know what they are. You've seen the shiny 3-D photos on some credit cards and a couple of the *National Geographic* covers, right? Well, that kind is kid stuff. The real thing is two or more photo images, taken from different but very precise angles and projected from exactly those same angles onto a glass surface. Say it's a photo of a glass of water, O.K.? When the two images come together, if it wasn't for the projector and sheet-of-glass setup, and if you don't move too far to one side or the other, you'd swear the water glass was there, right in front of your nose, and that you could reach out, pick it up, and drink it down.

Anyhow, by the time I drove out Bowdoin Street and up to the lab it was nine o'clock. I had fifteen minutes to pry the Professor loose. Which was going to take some doing.

He didn't hear me come in. Woody Newburger, the only cleaner the Professor allowed past the front door of his research labs, was running the vacuum in Lab A.

With all that noise, the little *Bzzzt!* that sounded after I tapped out the combination of the door to Lab B got drowned out. Once in, I saw that Professor Poplov wasn't at the Lab B computer after all. So he had to be in C, the big inner lab. Probably working at the control console for the projectors. I entered the number code for the lock on the small panel beside the heavy door, and swung it open.

And froze. The big, odd-looking gizmo the Professor was fiddling with was weird enough, but as I looked past to the hologram projection circle, I thought I must be seeing things.

Because there on the round, raised platform of the projection field, *I* stood with an armload of books, staring nervously back at me.

2

Professor Poplov touched a switch and the image vanished. When I managed to get a word out, it came in this embarrassing little-kid squeak. "Fantastic! How did you *do* that?"

The Professor looked as rattled as if he'd been caught out in the middle of the university quadrangle in his birthday suit. Turning away, he steered the bulky, five-foot-wide, seven-foot-high, humming whatsis on roller feet—with a cluster of what had to be klaser-gun barrels on its front—back across the floor and into the big, steel-doored storage vault he called Pandora's Cupboard. Nobody, but *no*body had ever seen him open those doors. I craned for a better look, but the Professor was too quick. With a twist he uncoupled the power cable, stowed it away, slammed the door, and punched the reset button on the security-lock panel.

So. He was working on two free-standing hologram projects at once. In one split second I saw it all, and my stomach dropped into my socks. One project would go belly-up once the other proved a success, and from the glimpse I'd had of what the whatsis—might as well call it Pandora's Box, since he kept it in Pandora's Cupboard—could do, it looked for sure like Pandora's Box was Project A and I was stuck with Project B.

Great. Just great. So what would I have to show for my two years of computing the Imager's lattices and angles, of doing the precision machine-shop work the Professor wouldn't trust to outsiders, of brewing tea and cleaning Lab C because Woody couldn't be trusted not to stumble over a cable or knock against a control switch? Nothing. No Ph.D. thesis on *Problems in Shifting Multiple-Lattice Integration Programming,* no valuable computer program. No degree. I'd have to start all over again with a new research project.

The Professor bustled past me.

"Do not bother me with questions. It is nothing. A fluke."

A fluke? Oh, sure, I thought. Tell me another one. The odds against that's being true had to be millions to one.

"Why, J. J.," the Professor went on grumpily, "do you not announce over the loudspeaker before you are coming in? How many times do I tell you always that you must do so? What is in Pandora's Cupboard is nobody's business but my own. Why else do you think I have called it that?"

I had always figured he'd called it that because he'd mixed up the tale of Bluebeard's cupboard with the old Greek legend of Pandora's box. And because both the grisly cupboard and the awful box were off limits to all comers. But what Pandora's lifting her box's lid and letting loose a swarm of troubles on the world had to do with anything Professor Poplov might be working on was a puzzle to me.

He hooked his thumbs in his belt and glowered at me over his gold-rimmed eyeglasses. His short, full beard and halo of fine, white hair bristled, and in his red-checked shirt, brown cord trousers, and Beanboots, he looked like a bad-tempered out-of-uniform Santa Claus.

"When I order, it is for a good reason," he growled. "So?"

"I'm very sorry, sir. I was in a hurry. I—"

"It is not like J. J. Russell to hurry." Professor Poplov frowned at his watch. "Hah! You are nine whole minutes late. To hurry would make you on time, not late."

Me late? I opened my mouth, but then shut it again. Professor Poplov was touchy, and I needed to keep on his good side. If the Imager *did* go down the drain, there might still be work I could do on his Project A, whatever it was. Or something new, if it came to that. Face it, even without Pandora's Box, I had problems. My research on the Imager looked as if it could drag on for another year thanks to the Professor's habit of coming up with "interesting little problems" to sidetrack me. Step on his corns, and I might not be "Doctor" Russell before I was twenty-five. I couldn't risk that. Polly would be graduating from college in just over three years. According to my master plan, by then I ought to be out on my own and raking in enough money from new inventions to have a twelve-cylinder Jaguar and a house in Shady Oaks Estates with a swimming pool, and marry Polly in Trinity Cathedral up in the city. I kind of liked the university chapel, but Polly said the cathedral is classier. She knows all that kind of stuff.

When I reminded Professor Poplov about the conference and his eleven-o'clock flight to Geneva, he did apologize. And we did get off in pretty good time. The Professor drove, and talked nonstop the whole way. Mostly it was stuff he'd forgotten to tell me to do while he was away, and about the only time I managed to wedge a word in sideways, I wished I hadn't.

"I do think I ought to inform you, sir, that the campus police have reason to believe that a would-be intruder attempted to breach lab security last night."

"*What?*" The word came out in a shout and Professor Poplov raised his hands from the steering wheel in alarm.

I grabbed it just in time. "N-nothing actually h-happened," I wheezed as we narrowly missed drifting into the side of a monster moving van. "But something did trigger the alarm."

The Professor took over the wheel again and hunched forward, scowling. "Which alarm?"

"Lab C, sir. But I assure you no one got in. I was sleeping in the middle lab. And the police were quite thorough. They inspected each of the windows and the ventilation apparatus on the roof, and found no evidence of an attempt at a forced entry."

The Professor, distracted for a moment from his pet worry, sighed. "Must you always talk like the butler in a British detective film, J. J.? And you are wearing a tie in the middle of Tuesday morning! Four years ago, yes, I can see that such formalities would make a twelve year old feel not a child. But now! Now you are not yet seventeen and already you are older than I. Such a pity!"

I didn't pay much attention to all that, coming as it did from a world-famous scientist setting off for a formal reception and conference in Geneva, Switzerland, in an old flannel shirt and Beanboots. Especially considering that he has been speaking English ever since he and his folks left Russia more than forty years ago, and he still has an accent and can turn out sentences shaped like pretzels. It only shows how little he cares about having a polished public image.

Image. The thought reminded me. "Sir? Your suit is in the garment bag, and your black shoes and socks and some white shirts in the carry-on case. And a suitable tie. There may not be time to change in the airport, but you *must* change. Can you manage it in one of the lavatories on the plane? I know it will be awkward, but you really must try," I pleaded. Not that I had much hope he'd remember.

"Ah, hrm!" he snorted. "If I must, I must. Yes, yes, I promise. But you must promise something to me, also."

"Promise what?" I slid him an uneasy look. Promise not to peek into Pandora's Cupboard? If I did sneak a peek and he found out, I'd be out on my ear like Max Sharp, the research assistant before me who got caught programming the lab's new supercomputer to play Adventure. Professor Poplov had never trusted a one of his past research assistants or graduate students with the cupboard's combination. For all I had ever known, he could have been working all along on something really wild. Some gizmo out of "Star Trek." What I did know was that it wasn't a government project. Or a university one either. He'd never tell the university what he was up to in the Poplov Labs, because as of two years ago they refused to cough up any more money for his independent research. Most of what he spent came out of the pot of gold some invention or other earned him—probably the PowerJack, that shoebox-size power generator-intensifier.

The Professor nodded briskly. "You will sleep again in the lab. Every night until my return. We take no chances. Every motion picture and communications company would like to put their greedy hands upon our Imager. If they knew we were making such a thing, they would swoop down upon us like a flock of crows."

"I hardly think you need worry, sir," said I. "Not with such an efficient electronic hedge around the building."

He gave me a stern look. "Once upon a time, Mister Russell, I too trusted in locks, but I tell you—"

I never heard what it was he meant to tell me because just then we hit the airport turnoff and had to concentrate on parking, checking the Professor in, and getting him on the right plane. If I'd left him to board by himself, he would probably have wandered onto the first flight called, and ended up in Sydney, Australia.

I hung around until the plane took off, and still had an hour and a half before I was due at Polly's dorm. You know how something can be bothering you, and you decide you're imagining it because you can't think what on earth it is? Well, all the way home I had this feeling there was something I ought to remember. Something important. But at the same time I was worrying about whether Mom had remembered to get my best tie back from the cleaners, telling myself not to forget Polly's locket, and thinking maybe I should call up after all to make sure lobster tails were on the menu at the Gilded Shrimp. So whatever was niggling at me didn't get a chance to surface.

I got home with time enough to change clothes, but not to shower. So I splashed on lots of my dad's cologne. I had buttoned the clean shirt and was knotting my best tie when I looked over at the bed and saw—*really* saw—the tie I had been wearing since Monday morning. It lay on top of the shirt I'd slept in.

White shirt. Brown tie with thin cream-colored stripes.

And then I remembered this weird thing . . .

I remembered what I saw when I opened the door to the inner lab and looked at that hologram of myself in the projection field.

It had been wearing an old blue shirt and tartan tie that I'd grown out of three, maybe four years ago.

Before I came to work with Professor Poplov.

Before there *was* a holographic imager project.

3

Polly toyed with the last of her lobster. Her blue eyes kept drifting toward the little package wrapped with gold lace ribbon.

"Give me a hint," she coaxed. "Just a teeny one."

"Hint? About what?" I hadn't taken my eyes off her, but I was miles away, still baffled by that blue shirt and tartan tie. And when you can't keep your mind on Polly Armbruster, who as you may know is five-feet-four inches of A-plus blond, that's A-plus bafflement.

"About my present, silly," Polly urged. "What's the matter with you? For the last three minutes all you've done is stare a hole through my shoulder and push that poor scallop around your plate. Are you road-testing it to see how many miles it's good for?"

I frowned down at the scallop on my fork. It did look like it needed a retread. I ate it and put the fork down.

"I apologize, Apollonia. Professor Poplov has left me with an immense amount of work, not to mention a considerable conundrum. But you're right. I promise—"

Polly was already off on another tack. "I do wish you'd stop calling me Apollonia." She pouted. "It makes you sound so stuffy. And it makes me sound like a—a brand of fancy mineral water."

I stared. "But you have always insisted that you abominated 'Polly,'" I protested with all the dignity I could manage.

"And that's another thing—"

Polly put her fork down very gently, as if what she'd really like to do was throw it at the wall. Or stick it in my arm.

"What is 'another thing'?" I asked automatically. Not that I was sure I wanted to hear.

Polly took a deep breath. "Do you *always* have to sound as if all you eat for breakfast, lunch, and dinner is alphabet soup? 'Insisted'? 'Abominated'? The way you talk! It's like using a sledgehammer to drive tacks. What's wrong with 'said' and 'hated'? You know how smooth your friend Max Sharp is. Listen to him sometime."

Max Sharp was no friend of mine, but that wasn't what bothered me. I had this sudden weird feeling—like in a dream, where you open your bedroom window and instead of Melville Street, there's Antarctica. And you look down your front and your pajamas are gone and you're a penguin, all feathers and feet. *Is that what I look like?* you think in a panic. Who, me, stuffy? First Professor Poplov complains, and now Polly . . .

"But—" I tried not to sound as if she *had* skewered me with that fork. "You always said you liked the way I talked. You said I sounded—dignified. Distinguished."

Polly shrugged prettily. "I suppose I did. When I was in the ninth grade. It made you seem older than me. After all, you *were* a college man even if you did look like a seventh grader. I was impressed to pieces. I was the only girl at Locke Junior High who went to the movies Saturday afternoons with a college man."

"And now?"

"Well—" She gave me this funny look that for some reason reminded me of our cat, Ginger. "My freshman English professor calls it 'verbal overkill.' He says it's a sign of insecurity."

Me? John James Russell? Insecure? I just sat there and stared.

"*I* know you're not," Polly leaned across to whisper as the waiter cleared our plates. "But you wouldn't—*I* wouldn't like other people to think you are."

What could I say after that? That I will strive to accommodate myself to your preferences in the matter of diction? Would you believe, it took a real effort to come up with a plain old "I'll think about it." I was glad when we moved on to other things, like how soon I would finish my computer program for the holographic imager, and when I was sending my article on lattice-integration anomalies (don't worry—you don't need to remember, let alone know what it means) off to *Electro-Optics*. My ship, you could say, was on its way into harbor.

When our pieces of strawberry pie came, Polly's was topped off with a birthday candle. I was kind of sorry it was too fancy a place for all the waiters to come over and sing "Happy Birthday." But then Polly would have thought that too corny for words—which might be one reason she picked the Gilded Shrimp instead of the Happy Tureen or the Green Pagoda.

Polly finished off two pieces of strawberry pie and then, while we were waiting for our coffee, walked her fingers across the tablecloth to pounce on the little gold-ribboned package.

"I love presents."

My mom always unties gift-wrap ribbons carefully and rolls them up to use again. Not Polly. She tears them off and rips through the paper like a little kid.

"A jeweler's box—oh, J. J., you *shouldn't* have!"

I grinned—pretty sappily, I guess. "I don't know why not."

"Oh." Polly looped a forefinger in the chain to lift the gold heart out of the box. She looked at it for a moment.

"What a cute little diamond."

That, I have to admit, gave me a twinge. Six hundred and seventy-five dollars, and she makes it sound like "What a cute little pencil case." But she did put it on, and every waiter in the Gilded Shrimp was looking at her as if she were a strawberry pie supreme. If I were a balloon I'd have burst, I was so proud.

And if I were a balloon I couldn't have floated much higher than I did all the way back to Polly's dorm. When we got there she gave me a peck on the cheek and dashed off to change for her two-o'clock tennis class. On my way back to the car I picked up a newspaper as I floated past the *Campus Daily* rack. All I can say is, it's a good thing

I didn't look at it then. Instead of turning down Old College Way I might have headed left up the hill and off the dock into Paradise Pond. Well—maybe not, since it wasn't my car. Besides, with Paradise Pond, before you got in deep enough to drown your misery, you'd be stuck up to your axles in mud.

I don't actually remember driving to the lab, but I got there. Woody Newburger's beat-up old Chevy pickup was still in the lot. Woody was sitting behind the wheel, singing to himself and sipping away at a bottle in a sack. His dark hair flapped lankly over his forehead and he looked more of a mess than usual. Two-day beard, dirty denim shirt, grubby cords, ratty tennis shoes. The white lab coat he wore at work was always clean and freshly ironed, but somehow that only made him look more disconnected. That and his permanently astonished eyebrows, and the way he carried on philosophical discussions with Fred, his pet rat, who rode in the lab coat's breast pocket.

Woody hadn't always been a cleaner. Up until about five years ago he'd been a lab assistant, and three years before that a research assistant. Everybody liked Woody. Last fall, Professor Poplov bullied the rest of the electrical engineering faculty into chipping in enough money to send him off to get dried out. He hadn't stayed dry for long.

I reached in across the passenger seat and snagged the keys out of the ignition before old Woody lowered the sack and saw me.

"Hey, iss ol' J. J." He beamed, focusing his pale blue eyes on me with an effort, and then suddenly looked as if he might cry. "'Sawful news, innit? Stinkin.' You gonna be O.K., Johnny boy?"

"I don't know what you're groaning about, Woody. I'm fine. Never better."

"Thass right. Stiff upper lib." Woody hiccupped. "Not me. Cried when I saw page three. Same thing happen t' me once. Know jus' how you feel. Here, have a swig, li'l buddy."

"Me? No thanks, Woody. I've got work to do." I didn't have a clue what he was talking about, and decided he didn't either. So I gave him a wave as I backed off, and hurried on into the building. As soon as I let myself into Lab A, I phoned Woody's sister to come get him. Then I tilted my desk chair back and opened the *Campus Daily*. The world still had this nice, rosy glow left over from my lunch with Polly, and I didn't much feel like brooding about some mysterious gizmo in the Professor's cupboard, let alone like settling down to work.

The headlines were your typical *Campus Daily* assortment. TUPPERMAN NAMED RHODES SCHOLAR. LIBRARY'S COMPUTERIZED CHECKOUT SYSTEM GOES ON-LINE. ENVIRONMENT SECRETARY TO ADDRESS GRADS. GRAFFITI ARTIST STRIKES AGAIN. And E. E. GRAD STUDENT HITS JACKPOT.

Electrical engineering graduate student? Who? It sure wasn't me. I sat up straight and read on.

E. E. GRAD STUDENT HITS JACKPOT

Galaxitronics Research Corporation announced Saturday that they have acquired the rights to the Compat translator chip designed by graduate electrical engineering student *(continued on Page 3)*

I turned the page so fast it tore.

> Maxwell Sharp. The Compat—short for "compatibility"—program not only allows computers programmed in different computer languages or with different protocols to communicate, but it . . .

But it also sank that ship I told Polly would be coming in before the end of the semester.

I didn't need to read the rest of the half-page article. I had been so sure my Translat (short for "translator") program was going to make me a mint that I'd promised Polly I'd get a car. A Jaguar X12, I said. Like the one in the Motor World display window she had been sighing over for the past five months. And now Translat was down the tubes! For the past year I'd spent all my free time—when I wasn't with Polly, that is—on my own program chip, and now Max the Shark had beaten me to it. Max was living proof, I thought glumly, of the old saying, "Them as has, gets." He was rich, brainy, and girls followed him around like he was some kind of Pied Piper in Ray-Bans and Reeboks.

O.K. These things happen, I told myself.

It didn't help much. My stomach still felt like a blender somebody'd turned from stir up to mix.

It's true, though. These things do happen. All the time. An idea's in the air, and maybe a dozen people from here to India up and decide to work on it. It happened to Woody Newburger back when he was a grad student. The week before he was to turn in his Ph.D. dissertation, *Electronic Frontiers* published an article by some guy in

Rhode Island who'd picked exactly the same research project. And got there first. So that was what Woody meant by "Know jus' how you feel."

But it wouldn't be as hard on me. The job Woody had lined up with Galaxitronics fell through because he didn't get the degree, and his girl walked out on him. That's what flattened him. I was lucky. The Translat chip wasn't my main project, and Polly wasn't Woody's Doris. "Doris the Deserter" was what everybody called her when they talked about her behind Woody's back.

Right then, wouldn't you know it, was when I spotted the two-column box in the *Personals* section at the bottom of the page.

LOVELY LONI . . . HAPPY 18th!
Tonite's the Night!
Love, MAX

Max the Shark was at it again. After the story about Galaxitronics and his Compat chip, I was surprised he hadn't signed it Supermax. Loni, whoever she was, was sure to be a foxy blond, the latest in old Max's long line of them.

Foxy blond?

Loni . . .

I do wish you'd stop calling me Apollonia.

Happy 18th.

Happy Birthday . . .

No, it couldn't be.

4

Oh, yes it could.

What I did was, I phoned Polly's Granny Armbruster down in Gilroy to "leave a message." Pretty crafty. The trouble was, it worked. Sure enough, Polly wasn't expected for any family birthday supper. Old Mrs. Armbruster hadn't seen her since last Christmas, and didn't expect to before the next one.

I sat there feeling like I'd been skewered with a—a laser beam. Like I had this round hole right through where my heart used to be.

Polly, how could you? *Max Sharp!*

There had to be some mistake. Had to be. *Had* to be. Maybe the party she said she was going to was a surprise family get-together *for* her granny in Gilroy. Why hadn't I thought of that before? Of course that was it.

I looked at my watch. Five to three. Plenty of time. If I used the car, parked on Old College Lane and walked the rest of the way, there was a bench under the trees in Powell Grove that overlooked the dorm parking lot where Polly parked her Honda. If she got out of class at ten to three, it would take at least half an hour for her to get back to the dorm and change. She couldn't be ready to leave for home—or Gilroy, if she wasn't going home first—before three-twenty.

This is really embarrassing. Humiliating. But what can I say? I went. I went, and I sat on the bench behind the manzanita bushes in Powell Grove for over an hour with my eyes glued to the new little yellow Honda, license number 9HMK600. Polly hated its being a Honda—to Polly anything less than a T-Bird was the pits—but her father wasn't exactly rich, and living in the dorm wasn't exactly cheap. Especially when, as her dad said, she had a perfectly good bedroom at home, less than two miles away.

Well, she never came near the Honda.

As luck would have it, I could see across the parking lot to the sidewalk in front of the dorm. Some luck! I sat there and saw Polly—*my* Polly, go sailing down the dorm's front steps in a blue dress and a long, spangly scarf and step into a shiny black—you guessed it—Jaguar X-JS. With Max Sharp holding the door for her. The last I saw of her as the Jag vroomed out of sight in the general direction of the city was a spangly flutter of scarf.

The next thing I remember, I was sitting in front of my Lab B computer terminal, swiveled around in the chair, watching Fred the rat walk in through the open door from Lab A. I remember thinking Woody must have hung up his lab coat somewhere with Fred still in the pocket.

I don't remember Inch One of that drive back to the Poplov Labs. I only know I drove because I found the

Professor's Volvo in the lab parking lot afterward. Me, I was paralyzed from the eyebrows up. My heart was broken. So? So don't even think about it, I told myself in despair. Think about something else. Anything.

So I did. I have this knack. I can shut things off. If I really want to concentrate, I can shut out hard rock, construction work, my mom yelling at me—anything.

I chucked the *Campus Daily* in the wastebasket, scooped up Fred, stuck him in my jacket pocket, and headed for the Lab C door. The lunch at the Gilded Shrimp had put it right out of my mind, but when I opened that door six-plus hours earlier, something very weird had been going on. Well, now I meant to find out what.

What was weirdest of all, I'd remembered the hologram image hadn't seemed as close-up as it should, and had finally figured out why. I didn't *look* smaller in it. I *was* smaller. The top one of those books I saw me clutching? I hadn't seen it very clearly in the second or two before the image was gone, but from the pattern on the dust jacket I could've sworn it was *Brainwaves*, that book Professor Poplov wrote eight or so years ago about the world's seven most important inventions. Well. It was *Brainwaves* that convinced me I ought to be a rich scientist instead of a rich toy inventor. I brought it to the Professor's lab my first week at the university to ask him to sign it. "What am I—a pop star, that you should ask me such a thing?" is what he said. But he signed it. It's been up in my room in that old glass-fronted bookcase ever since.

Ever since I was twelve.

And that old blue shirt and the tartan tie I told you I'd grown out of? Mom gave them to the Goodwill, I think. The tie was a birthday present from Granny Allen, and the last time I tried it on—two years ago?—it was so short it didn't reach to the bottom of my breastbone. That photo on our mantelpiece downstairs at home of me in my high-school graduation cap and gown? I'm wearing it in that. That was four years ago. And four years back, Professor Poplov was still working on the hyperlaser (klaser to you) that gave him the first idea for the Poplov fiber-optical K-laser microprojector (another mouthful you don't need to remember) and afterward our imager system.

Sure, I'd recognized myself standing on the projection field. But the reason I looked small hadn't been because it was an image photographed from a distance. It was because I was a junior edition of me: the twelve-year-old college man.

And alarm system or no, I had to find out how the Professor had done it.

5

Half an hour later, I was more puzzled than ever. There wasn't even a snapshot of me listed in the lab's computerized image index, and certainly no twenty-four films of me for the twenty-four camera angles we used to make a free-standing hologram. The answer was sitting inside Pandora's Cupboard, but just peering at its doors was enough to give me Jell-O knees. I decided instead to have a look at what our Imager could do now that I'd debugged another section of the computer program. If it was good enough, and if I worked like mad to get the rest of the bugs out, why couldn't it be as good or better than Pandora's Box? Why risk everything, asked the chicken in me, just to solve some minor mystery?

I pulled the cassettes of a demonstration film we'd shot—one of the Professor explaining the projection system—and loaded them on a trolley cart. After making sure the doors of the two outer labs were locked and the alarms set, I unlocked the door to Lab C and wheeled in the film trolley.

The Imager's projection field—a black, circular platform six feet across with a wide raised rim that concealed the low-level projectors—and the big, clear glass cylinder that lowered from above to rest on the outer rim hadn't been fiddled with. The projection angles are controlled by computer, and the readout checked O.K. The film console along the wall, with its cables looping down and snaking across the floor, looked the same as it had since we hooked it up back around Christmastime. And when I put the cassettes in the numbered slots and typed out LOAD DEMO ^@/A7&!*, the glass cylinder eased on down and, inside it, the old familiar Poplov blur appeared on the platform. Oh, it was a bit sharper than a week ago, but after you've made half a notebook full of computer-program corrections, you hope you'll be dazzled by the improvement. But, no. Sure, when the fuzzy figure on the platform raised both hands and announced over the stereo speakers, "*My esteemed colleagues, ladies and gentlemen, thank you for your most kind attention,*" anybody would have recognized Professor Poplov. But a blur is a blur is a blur. Stepping carefully over the heavy cables that snaked across the floor, I walked around him—it. And the news wasn't all bad. In the middle of his back—the last segment I had worked on the night before—the pattern of his plaid shirt was actually almost in focus.

But almost wasn't good enough. Almost was still months away from good enough. And the thing—I had started to think of it as "the Box"—in Pandora's Cupboard had produced a fully three-dimensional image of that twelve-year-old me in what looked like perfect focus. Face it. The Professor's secret machine was a hands-down winner. The Imager was a dead duck. And so was I. Two years of hard work down the tubes. No project. No degree next year. No pots of money to follow.

And, twittered a nasty little voice at the back of my mind, *No forty-thousand-dollar Jaguar. No Apollonia.*

Well, I thought, after sitting there glumly for ten minutes, if my world was going to fall apart anyhow, at least I could satisfy my curiosity about the Box.

The trouble was, only Professor Poplov knew the combination for the electronic lock on Pandora's Cupboard. With his bonnet so full of bees on the subject of security, you could be sure that if you entered the wrong number, your own was up. And, though the big storage vault was such a deep, dark secret that its combination panel probably wasn't wired into the main alarm system that set off gongs or buzzers or whatever in the campus police office, there had to be some backup protection. Odds were the lab was booby-trapped. Right then I didn't care much. So what if a steel-mesh net drops down on me from a ceiling compartment? Or if the computer overrides all the door locks in the building so I'm trapped? That would be more the Poplov style. Neat, not flashy. With nothing to eat but the last of a bag of gummy bears that had been in my desk since Christmas, I'd be in great shape by the time he got back on the weekend. But then, what did I care?

I can hear you say it—revise the window-alarm program on the computer, dummy, and open a window for an escape hatch. But that was much too easy. Professor Poplov would have set up an override alarm to protect the system from changes. No. If anybody was going to get into Pandora's Cupboard for a look at the Box, it would be with the combination. Fat chance. Do you know how many possible six-digit combinations there are? Too many and then some. And Professor Poplov wouldn't have it written down anywhere even though his memory did sometimes need jogging. Oh, he can keep an almost endless string of equations in his head. And reeling off the value of π—*pi* to you fuzzies who don't know any math—is his idea of a party trick. A piece of pie, excuse the pun. He can rattle off 3.141592653589793 and keep on going as long as anybody wants to stand around and listen. But if a number doesn't *mean* anything—if it was given out eeny-meeny-miny-mo, like, say, a telephone number—he can look it up in the phone book and forget the last half before he's finished dialing. He wouldn't remember his own phone number, which is 123-0270, if the first six digits weren't the same as 12/30/27, his birthdate. That he remembers.

So how did he keep from forgetting the combination to Pandora's Cupboard? Maybe by using a mathematical formula. To start with, you could rule out the first six digits of old *pi*, or of any long or infinite series. Their point was that they *did* go on and on. So what—

That's when it hit me. Why only six digits? So what if the other electronic locks on campus used six? There was no reason why an electronics whiz like Professor Poplov couldn't, with a bit of tinkering, expand the lock's combination as much as he wanted.

Me, I was shaky on *pi* once I got past the thirtieth digit, so I trotted back out to the terminal in the outer lab and loaded the Basic Math Review program from the university computer's memory. Then I printed out as much of the value of *pi* as I could stand still to wait for, and ripped off the printout to hurry back to Lab C. The red light on the security lock panel beside the doors to Pandora's Cupboard glared its beady little warning at me, but I took a deep breath, bit my lip hard, and pushed the first buttons. 3-1-4 . . .

Nothing happened. No bells, no sirens. No steel cage dropped from the ceiling. I tried to keep tapping the digits out as quickly as I would for any security lock, but it wasn't easy. The buttons are as small as the ones on a pocket calculator. What if I hit the wrong one? Besides, after the first dozen or so numbers I had to keep looking back and forth from the printout to the number panel, just to be safe.

1-5-9-2-6-5-3-5-8-9-7-9-3-2-3-8 . . .

Still nothing. But why should there be? The alarm could be clanging away down in the campus police office, not in the lab. In two minutes I'd hear sirens screaming into the parking lot for sure. 8-8-4-1-9-7-1-6-9-3-9-9 . . .

And then it opened.

Snick. Just like that. Seven digits short of the end of my *pi* printout. Seven digits more and the old fox would have got me. That would have worried me if I hadn't been in such a fever of curiosity. It should have worried me. Almost anybody who knew Professor Poplov could have figured out that combination. If nobody had, it was only because nobody knew there might be something very interesting in Pandora's Cupboard. After his independent research funds were cut off, the Professor had done without lab assistants in Lab C. For the past two years I'd been the only one allowed past that door.

Anyhow, there it sat. Professor Poplov's whatsis-machine. The Box.

Now, if I do say so myself, I've got a fairly good set of equipment between my ears. I'd told myself that I knew enough about the Professor's past work and the way his mind ticks for me to tell what sort of imager the Box was once I got a good, close look at it. But it didn't look like anything I'd ever seen before. Even after I wheeled it out—it must have weighed a ton, but moved easily enough on its roller feet—even after I wheeled it out into the fluorescent glare of the lab and inspected it from all sides, it was beyond me. Its back side was a console panel with dials and meters and digital counters, and one of the new HP Mini-Zylox supercomputers. With a little monster number cruncher like that, no matter how complicated the Box was, there'd be no need to tie into the university's big mainframe computer. One of the Box's side panels was off, and here and there in the spaghetti-tangle of wiring and ribbon cables, I spotted complicated fittings and other bits of hardware I'd made myself. Bits I'd machined according to Professor Poplov's drawings. Bits from some project he later said hadn't worked out. As for what the Box looked like, there's no point going into a lot of detail. Just picture a weird lumpy gizmo about five feet wide on each side and seven feet high, with what looked like twelve klaser-gun barrels sticking out at the front—three tight vertical rows of four. Whatever it was, at least I could tell what it wasn't. It wasn't anything to do with 3-D holography. Not with those klasers bunched that close together.

The power cable leading to Pandora was as thick as my wrist—a good three times heavier than anything we used on the Imager. I'd seen Professor Poplov disconnect it, so didn't have any trouble finding the removable panel in the metal-grid floor. But when I lifted the grid clear and saw the mark stamped beside the power socket and on the double-safety cable clamps, it was like somebody'd laid an ice-cold hand on the back of my neck. . That was the logo of Galaxitronics—the big research complex up in the industrial park on the hill up back of the campus. It was called the Brain Bin back when it was started up fifteen or twenty years ago right here in our building by a bunch of professors who were into high-energy physics. Professor Poplov and some of the others dropped out when the group decided to set up as a private company and buy the property they'd leased for two or three years up on Humboldt Hill. After they moved the whole operation up there, they got into top-secret research. And they are *rich*. The buzz now is that they're working toward a gamma-ray laser. One of those babies has got to take something like eighty or a hundred trillion watts of power. You can't just pump one up with some old eximer and carbon-dioxide laser. Or even a K-laser. It would take the kind of power you get from nuclear fusion. Not "fission," like in atomic explosion. Fusion. More an implosion ("unplosion" to you?) than an explosion. Kind of—oh, forget it. Just a

dim idea of all those watts will do you. Try imagining all of the electrical power in the world zapping—for only a shaving of a second—one gummy bear. *Bzmt.*

And my Professor Poplov had fiddled a way to bleed Galaxitronics power out through one of their old cables? Wow.

At the thought of all that power my hands went so sweaty and my fingers so spaghetti-limp that it took me half a dozen tries to get the cable fitted into the power couple and locked fast. It wasn't that I was scared. The thought of a power surge and me being broiled to a crackling never crossed my mind. I was too excited—in fact, just about foaming at the mouth. All that ran through my idiot pea brain was *Oh-man-oh-man-oh-man, what does this blithering box of bits and bolts DO? What's it FOR?*

I think maybe I had a glimmer even then. But how could I admit such a nutty thing to prim, precise, practical J. J. Russell?

It wasn't until I went back to the Box to switch on the power that I spotted the disk in the computer drive. Where I should have looked first, of course. Which just shows to go you, to bend a phrase, what shape I was in. Anyway, there it was. If Professor Poplov hadn't been so rattled when I walked in on him, and if I hadn't been in such a twist about getting him to the airport on time, he would have locked the program disk up as usual in his private safe.

I pulled a chair up to the control keyboard, switched on, held my breath, and entered POPLOVLAB C LOAD:MENU.

And there it was. No need for you to bend yourself around the technical jargon, but it began

MASTERFILE EDWFR: EXPERIMENTS IN DECAYED WAVE FRONT RECOVERY

10 LAPSED-LIGHT SENSOR INTERPRETATION
70 SEQUENTIAL ULTRASENSING PROGRAM
220 COMPUTER ENHANCEMENT
380 . . .

That's as far as I got before the decayed wave front bit really hit me. Say you want to photograph a wave front—that's the light that bounces off an object—as the first step in making a holograph of whatever-it-is. O.K.? Well, a "decayed" wave front would be one that had bounced off the whatever-it-is *before* you took the photograph. It bounces, then breaks up.

Which meant . . .

People are always calling this or that "mind-boggling." Well, for the first time in my life I understood bogglement. More boggled than my mind you could not get. The Box—no joke—seemed to be claiming it could pick up and reconstruct the broken light waves. That it could take a picture now, this instant, of what had happened five minutes ago.

Even—if I'd seen this morning what I thought I saw—*even of what had happened five years ago.*

Impossible.

Of course it was impossible.

Of course.

6

You think that was crazy? When I displayed a couple of the programs on the monitor screen, not one of them looked like it could make the Box do what the function menu said it would. But I couldn't be sure, because to tell the truth I couldn't make head or tail of any of it. What it looked like was that the whole thing might be a code for something even weirder. And I couldn't get a handle on it any old where. That was spooky. After all, when it comes to computer programming, I'm supposed to be a real whiz. Complicated math? Piece of cake. Statistics? Strawberry cheesecake. So I should have been able to understand *some*thing of what was really going on in the program that told the Box how to do what it did. But I didn't. It was too long and too complicated a tangle. For all I knew it could be backwards, with some kind of hidden correction command. I knew that when it came to computer entry protocols and coded "locks," Professor Poplov was a pro's pro, but when the whole *program* is a lock—that's real Art with a capital A. Making sense of it (if I could) would take more like six months than the week I had before he got back.

But with what I had seen, I couldn't just leave it at that, now could I? O.K., so—

So what next? Switch the Box on and stand back?

Between Polly and the incredible Box I was so bent out of shape that I thought, *Well, and why not?* Hadn't I already gone too far to be worrying about what Professor Poplov would say?

Heavy as it was, the Box moved easily on its rollerball wheels. When I had it aimed where the Professor had aimed it—at the Imager's projection-field platform—I sat down at the controls keyboard at the back and nervously pecked out a command to run the EDWFR program.

ALL FUNCTIONS? asked the monitor screen.

What the heck? YES.

MINUS? the screen asked.

MINUS 4 YEARS, I typed back at it. I was itching for another look at that four-years-ago me.

Nothing happened. Except maybe the lab seemed a little—lighter. It wasn't a power surge. When I got up from the control console to check the power-monitor board and see why the glass projection cylinder hadn't come down, I looked over and saw this—this *bright* spot above the projection-field platform. More than a spot. More like a patch of light the shape of a six-foot-tall egg, hovering over the middle of the platform. Sort of. It was as bright as—well, about as bright as the whole lab is around noontime, with the sun coming in. And inside it, at the bottom, the middle of the platform *had no—middle.*

There was this yard-wide hole in it. Like a monster doughnut.

You could see down through to the floor.

And sitting in the doughnut hole was this ordinary old lab stool.

The same ordinary old lab stool—with the same old strip of green plastic tape on its black plastic seat—*that I had just been sitting on at the controls of the Box.*

The same, except the patch looked new.

"Oh, wow," I wheezed. Then I think I moaned and oh-wowed again. If you're anything like me, just when you think it would take whole paragraphs of six- or eight-syllable words to explain a whirly jumble of thoughts, all you can say is "Oh, wow!"

I should have seen Snag One right there, but I didn't.

Whether the bright scrap of a scene hovering in the projection field was four years or even four days ago, it was still incredible. Since it seemed to be midday there —*then,* I mean—the Box's measurement of time was a bit off. But that, as the Professor would have said, was a mere bagatelle.

Right about then is when I found out I hadn't guessed the half of it.

Who knows why I did what I did next? It was dumb. And it could have been The End for Fred, Woody's rat. I'd forgotten he was still in my jacket pocket. I guess he'd finished off all the crumbs in there, because he stuck his nose out, looked around, whiskers a-twitch, and gave me his beadiest "What's up?" look.

That look was his big mistake.

I picked him up by the tail and set him down at the edge of the projector-field platform. "See for yourself," I said.

See for yourself, my foot. "Show *me*." I don't remember, but I'll bet you I was doing the whole Mad Scientist bit, hunched over, rubbing the old hands, eyes burning. *Go, small Fred. Slip across the Great Divide and return to tell us of the Wonders Beyond.*

Serve me right if the little guy had skittered off and five minutes later strolled back wearing a mysterious rat smile.

Anyhow. There Fred sat. Then his whiskers trembled, his nose lifted as if it caught a familiar scent, and he scuttered off into the brightness. The last I saw of him was the twitch of the tip of his tail as the rest of him vanished down that weird doughnut hole in the platform.

I felt like a real crumb. What was I thinking of? I had zapped old Woody's best friend. For all I knew, the Box might have fried the poor little guy. Or bent his chromosomes. I watched the circle of floor visible under the stool in that Other Time, but he didn't cross it. Still, he *could* be O.K. He had probably fallen (I told myself), or maybe jumped, from the here-and-now platform onto the here-and-then floor and headed for cover.

I circled the platform in a panic. "Here, Fred! Good Fred! Where are you, Fred?"

He still wasn't anywhere in sight on what I could see of the floor-that-was, but that didn't have to mean he'd been, well, erased, did it? I felt awful. Sure, Fred was a nuisance sometimes. He and his neat little rat packets had no business being in any of the labs let alone super-clean Lab C. But he was Woody's best friend, and I had just waved him off into the Great Unknown.

All this required a pause for serious thought. Besides,

I was starving. Excitement grabs me that way. So I hurried to the Box's control keyboard, exited from the EDWFR program, switched off, and went through to Lab A, making sure the doors locked behind me. I found half a package of tortilla chips and the last of my supply of gummy bears in my bottom desk drawer, and a can of root beer in the fridge where Professor Poplov keeps some of our delicate equipment alongside his jars of soupy ground-up health salad. There was half a jar of salad left over from Monday. It looked pretty revolting, but I was desperate, so I took that too. Then I sat myself down in the Professor's old swivel chair, propped my feet on his desk, and thought while I munched. Or tried to.

O.K., I thought. It looked as if Fred had been either (a) disintegrated, or (b) transported four years into the past. Right? If it was (a), I had murdered the little guy. Period. But if it was (b), then there ought to be some way to get him back. Well, *might* be.

How about tying a piece of cheese on the end of a string and dangling it over the edge of the—um, "hole"? Except, I reminded myself, I was fresh out of cheese. It would have to be a piece of tortilla chip. So I put the last chip back in the bag. O.K. Say food brought him back in range. How was a four-inch-long rat supposed to climb up onto an eighteen-inch-high platform he maybe couldn't even see from wherever he was?

I thought about making a cardboard ramp. Or a box trap on the end of string? So I could lower it onto the four-year-ago floor? A . . .

It was when I tipped my head back to finish off the

root beer that the old E. E. research teams photo on the wall caught my eye. It was from three years ago, and there I was at the end of the second row: still a midget, with Woody standing tall beside me. But where was the Old Sobersides frown I remembered? Why the look out of the corner of my eye and the smirk that looked like I could hardly keep from cracking up?

The answer was right up there beside me.

Two rats had stuck their heads up out of the pocket of Woody's lab coat and fixed the camera with a look of happy, beady-eyed surprise, as if the photographer had just yelled "Cheese!"

Two.

Not "too." Two as in one-two.

One was the same young Fred who'd always been in the photograph. The other was—I swear—the full-grown Fred I'd just lost.

And then, suddenly, I wasn't sure.

Maybe if I'd stopped right there and thought my way from A to B to Z, I could have saved myself a heck of a lot of trouble later. But I was a little bit scared and a lot confused. I wasn't used to feeling like I had oatmeal between my ears, and I didn't like it one little bit. You'll have to admit, all this *was* weird. And suddenly it was as if I'd had a—a memory glitch. I remembered *remembering* the one-Fred photograph, but—get this—I didn't exactly remember *it*. If you know what I mean. (If you don't, don't sweat it. You're no worse off than I was.) What I *seemed* to remember now was that back around the time when I first started work in the Poplov Labs, Woody had two rats: Fred Junior and Fred Senior. That the little one vanished. And that Woody had always figured the campus fire department cat got him. At the same time I remembered—there always being *only* one Fred.

Now, *don't panic.* And don't stop now. You'll strip your gears if you try to figure out the Great Fred Flap all at one go. Besides, if you're a trifle baffled, you can understand all the better how I felt. I ended up wondering whether discovering the Box had totally unhinged my mind. Had there always been two rats in the photo? Could I have *imagined* sending Fred pitter-patting into the Box's line of fire? What if he was still in my jacket pocket?

The jacket was hanging on the back of the Professor's swivel chair. I looked.

He wasn't.

I sat down, took a deep breath, and told myself I had to think this thing through logically. If right now I were a five-year-old rat, and I *in my five-year-old body* got zapped back four years, then I would find myself walking around in the past *in* that five-year-old body while—*while there's a one-year-old me already walking around.* O.K. Wild, but O.K. Next, say the one-year-old me gets crunched by a cat. So now there's just one of me. And I'm stuck there in the past, and have to live *through* those four whole years all over again, to get back to this very day I got zapped out of. O.K.? So. So what started out as a five-year-old body is now a nine-year-old body.

Weird.

The worrying question was, if Fred was a time traveler,

could he have changed anything in the past? Hardly, since he never seemed to do anything in life but eat and ride around in Woody's pocket. So—he must be around somewhere right now.

I jumped up, slammed out of the lab, down the hall, and out of the building.

Woody's sister hadn't come yet. His pickup was still in the parking lot and he was still in it, snoring gently. I reached in the window and gave his shoulder a shake.

"Woody? Wake up, Woody! C'mon, Woody—where's Fred?"

"Fred?" Woody stirred and squinted his eyes against the light. "Whassa matter? Wha' d'you want him for?"

"Never mind. Just tell me where he is. It's important."

"No need t' shout," Woody said. He drew himself up with great dignity and began patting one pocket after another, first in the old tweed jacket, then the T-shirt where pockets would be if T-shirts had pockets. Woody began to look worried, but just then Fred peered out through the lanky hair that hung down over Woody's jacket collar, and gave us the old "What's up?" look. He'd been asleep back there, I guess.

"Good ol' Fred. My best fren'," Woody said sentimentally. He held his hand up and Fred walked onto it.

It was Fred, O.K. He was a little bit frazzled, but I figured that was because we'd wakened him out of a sound sleep. He certainly *looked* like the old Fred. Except—I swallowed and tried to sound casual. "Uh—didn't you have another rat three or four years back, Woody?"

He nodded. "Yep. 'Nother Fred. Young one, zackly like this Fred. Got him 'fore this one turned up outa the blue."

I was staring at Fred like he'd just landed from Mars when I heard a car pull into the lot. I turned to see a red VW Rabbit, with Woody's sister, Elsie, at the wheel, pull in two spaces away. Woody looked past me, and shook his head sadly. He hiccuped.

"Here I thought now you been ditched, you'd unnastand how it is. Why'd you hafta call Big Sis, ol' buddy? Why not jus' lemme alone?"

I gave Elsie the keys to the pickup, and left her to it.

By the time I locked myself back in the lab, I had a bad case of the shakes. Staring at Fred eyeball to eyeball, I'd seen what hadn't been so before. The hair around his nose and mouth was gray. But then again, if you were a middle-aged rat you'd for sure turn gray if somebody up and tacked an extra four years on your life.

O.K., so I couldn't be sure that's what happened. And I couldn't know whether the Box did anything more than recapture a scrap of the past like some magic camera. But if it *could fiddle time itself*, and if I *had* zapped Fred back four years into his past, then (a) he had survived the trip, (b) he had actually met himself, and (c) for some rat reason of his own, coming up to this afternoon the second time around so to speak, he'd managed to stick close to Woody.

The whole thing was crazy. Right off the wall. Impossible.

Or was it? I mean, there's no law that says if you can

zap yourself back in time you have to pick a time before you were born. Is there? So, the Now-You would be back there *at the same time* as the Then-You.

The snag was that "if you can." The trouble was, I knew for a fact that travel back in time is impossible. Well, maybe not for a fact. For the Accepted Theory. Most of the scientists and philosophers I've read agree: time travel to the future is possible—in theory—but not to the past.

In a nutshell, the argument is that backward time travelers have to be aware before they leave Point A (present time) for Point B (past time) that they *must* one way or another arrive back at A—the original time, at the original place—or they *will never have been there to go back in time in the first place.* This is what you call a "causal loop." As in cause-and-effect. Then the theorists draw diagrams and babble on about things like how since it is a logical and physical impossibility to strike a match right now and have it light a fire an hour ago, a causal loop is therefore impossible. Sure, I know now that you could drive a ten-ton truck through the holes in that theory and some of the others, but in eighth grade, when I first read all that stuff, it really impressed me. But what does some nut trying to light a fire an hour ago have to do with time travel anyway? Sloppy logic, if you ask me. Even in the eighth grade I should have spotted that. If you complete a time loop, why should you have to repeat it? And why should you forget you'd gone back?

So if I was right about what I'd done to old Fred, he now had under his belt, so to speak, the smarts that went with four more years of experience. Plus everything he knew before I zapped him.

What I needed was a foolproof test. Something I could send back and . . . a paper! Sure. Some paper that had been in the lab files for more than four years. Something that wasn't important enough to be looked at again, so had just sat there, but was still something that anybody finding it on the floor wouldn't throw away. Most important of all, it had to be something that wouldn't change the least little thing in the past. That way, it couldn't end up changing my being right here, looking through the very same file.

A letter would be best. There wouldn't be more than the one copy of a letter. I finally picked one written on June 6, 1980, to Professor Poplov from Professor William Yerby at CalTech about a book the two of them were working on back then. Professor Poplov never threw Yerby's letters away, so if Pandora's Box *did* zap it back onto the past-time Lab C floor, it was bound to get picked up and stuck in the file again.

So when I rechecked the Yerby folder, there it would be—both of it.

No sooner said than perpetrated: back into Lab C, letter dropped on the projection platform, the Box switched on, EDWFR program booted up, "MINUS 1 YEAR" command entered and, once more, the space above the center of the platform slowly brightened. The queer lightness maybe wasn't as strong as before, but you could still see its edges clearly. I wondered what would happen if I stuck my hand in.

I didn't try it. I figured I might not get it back.

For a second, as the Box shifted into high hum, the letter just sat there in midair in the middle of the platform. Then, suddenly, it blew sideways out of sight, as if somebody had opened the year-ago door, and the letter had got caught in the draft. I stared after it for a minute, then switched the Box off and tore back out to Lab A and the file cabinets.

I've heard about people being numb with excitement. Well, paralyzed is what I was. It was like my brain was asleep. I could barely remember what I was looking for. My fingers too. I could hardly make them riffle through the letters, but in the end I got to the Yerby file. And there it—*they*—were.

CalTech letterheads. Identical dates. *Dear Nick, The proofs have come from the publisher, and I will send them on to you . . .* Exactly the same. Same little coffee splotch at the bottom. Even the same tiny flaws in the paper.

"Shazam!" I whispered. That, in case you're too culturally impoverished to know about comics, is what this little kid Billy Batson says when he wants to turn into Captain Marvel and cream the villains.

Cream . . .

Cream the villain.

Why not?

7

By five o'clock I had made up my mind.

I was going to go back in time, and warn myself—that younger me.

I would get word to the then-me to get on the ball or Max the Shark was going to cut me out with both Polly and Translat.

Crazy? Sure.

Sure. Putzing around with the Box's control program, I had found the full command menu. Given the right commands, it looked like Pandora's Box could focus on not just one but a series of different times, stopping at each one for however long you chose. So long as you knew precisely when the two times were going to touch next, it was only logical that you should be able to step *back* through the window (or whatever you want to call it) in time. Right? Right.

I figured four months ought to give me plenty of time. Besides, the further back I went, the more chance there would be that an accident or some dumb thing I did could change something important. I didn't want to come back from Then and find my Now even more mucked up than it was already. I did some quick figuring in my head. Today was Tuesday the twelfth, and four months ago, December twelfth, had been a Saturday, so the lab would be empty.

I programmed the Box to send me back four months into the past, hold for ten minutes while I put a spoke in the Shark's wheel, and—in case something went wrong and I overstayed the ten minutes—immediately reset itself and open up the time window at twelve hours past the first stop. By the time I finished, it was 5:10 and the machine's eerie hum was giving me a real case of the twitters. Even so, by then I was so fired up that I probably wouldn't have backed off even if you'd offered me Polly, a silver X-JS Jag and a forty-foot racing yacht. But it did feel kind of like I was getting ready to step off the edge of the world. I put on my blazer, tied my tie, and hoped it hadn't been too cold on December twelfth. 5:12. Twitters or no, I had to get going. I entered the final command, set the timer on my digital watch, crossed my fingers that the power from Galaxitronics Research hadn't cut out at five o'clock, and at 5:15, right on the dot, the space above the platform grew slowly brighter.

I pushed the button on my watch's timer. And then my knees almost gave out. In the end, I had to sit down and scrootch across the Edge. Don't laugh. *You* might have chickened out, period. But then, you might have looked before you leaped, so to speak.

Not me. No, right there J. J. Russell the whiz kid joined all the rest of the pea brains who rush in where angels fear to tread.

No joke.

* * *

All I can say is, it was weird. One minute I'm scrooching, the next I landed hard on the lab floor.

"Ow!"

I got up, rubbed my tailbone, and looked around.

Everything was so familiar that for a second it felt like nothing had happened. Nothing. Except, of course, that Pandora's Box was gone and the doors to the big steel storage cupboard were padlocked.

I had really done it!

I had done it, but I couldn't believe it. It was a good minute before I remembered to check the time. I had allowed myself ten minutes for leaving a message to me in a likely computer file. Make that nine minutes. I switched my watch from the timer to the chronometer. It read 5:16. Funny. Because the clock on the lab wall said 12:31 . . .

12:31. That would explain the midday sun that still slanted sharply in at the windows, and the bright sunshiny patch in the April afternoon light of the lab I'd come from. I'd been right. The Box's aim wasn't exactly bang on target. I didn't like that, but so long as I kept an eye on my watch, I ought to be O.K. I was too jacked up to worry.

Eight minutes and forty seconds.

I crossed to the door to Lab B, propped it open with a stool so I could get back through without being slowed by the lock, and made a beeline for my computer terminal. It was the only one tied in to the university mainframe computer, but even our low-security "locks" on the lab files—the access codes—were (knock on wood) as near foolproof as they can be. Once into my

Poplov Labs files, all I had to do was enter my "Things to Do" file code and then type out the warning: A WORD TO THE WISE: FINISH TRANSLAT QUICKLY. MAX SHARP IS DEVELOPING AN ALTERNATIVE SILICON-CHIP VERSION. AND HE HAS HIS BEADY EYE ON POLLY.

I thought for a long minute, then deleted the last sentence. It didn't sound like me. Too slangy. Undignified. Besides, better not even mention Polly. Upset the me-here-in-the-past, and I—*he*—might put our dumb foot right in it. Stir up seventy-six complications. I couldn't take the chance.

Six minutes and thirty-two seconds.

In a rush, I clacked away again at the keys: SAY NOTHING TO ANYONE—REPEAT, ANYONE. THAT OUGHT TO DO IT.

Funny, even while I was clacking away, I knew something was wrong. If I hadn't been in such a hot-eyed hurry, I would have noticed it first thing. But I didn't have just my ten-minute deadline to worry about. Sure it was a Saturday, but what if Professor Poplov turned up anyway? How did I know he hadn't? I came in on Saturdays a lot myself. What if that other me walked in on this me? Just thinking about it gave me the willies. Let the physicists and philosophers argue out what happens when you meet yourself. I wasn't about to be the one who found out the hard way.

I logged off, shut down the terminal, and checked my watch again. Four minutes to go. Buckets of time.

But when I got to the door of Lab C and saw that reassuring afternoon shadow in the noonday air, I slowed and then stopped.

I stopped because this little voice piped up inside my head . . .

"Where's the fire?"

Three and a half minutes.

Where *was* the fire?

I hesitated there, frozen with one foot in the air, like back when I was a little kid and we played statues.

Was there any fire?

Well, if there wasn't, there could be. I knew the only sensible thing was to get right back to Now. So I was going to. Had to. I took a halfhearted step toward the Box's time window.

Three minutes, thirteen seconds.

On the other hand, why rush off? If I stayed, I had twelve hours to play around with before the Box opened the window in time again. Why not—

I stood there and dithered until the timer on my watch went off. *Peep-peep-peep-peep-peep.*

The shadowy time window faded, and was gone.

Then, wouldn't you know, once it was too late, I had this horribilous sinking feeling. Kind of like you'd have on the way down if you hadn't checked to be sure there was water in the pool before you jumped off the high dive.

The wall clock said 12:40. I took a deep breath. O.K., Russell, pull yourself together and get a move on.

The two outer labs were clear. The hallway beyond was deserted too, except for a girl I saw vanish around the corner toward the front entrance. As soon as I heard the bang of the front door, I eased the Lab A door shut behind me, wincing as the lock snapped shut with a loud click. Then I took a deep breath and headed down the hall and around the corner with an I'm-going-to-be-late-to-wherever-I'm-going stride.

And ran smack into Woody Newburger.

Woody, in sad need of a haircut, but even so looking noticeably tidier than usual, was wheeling a dolly stacked with cartons of computer paper. I kept right on going, but he stopped dead. I could tell without turning around because there was this *thunk-thunk!* as a couple of cartons hit the floor. As the door swung shut behind me I snuck a quick look and saw him standing in the middle of the hall with one hand up. He had a startled, uncertain look. Kind of like a—a fuddled sheepdog. All I could think was that he had just seen me somewhere else. Which meant I needed to put as much distance as possible between me and the west campus science buildings. If I had been on campus this Saturday it could only have something to do with work. That meant the Poplov Labs, so the faster I got away, the better. I took off across the parking lot at full speed.

What did I think I was doing? Good question.

Sure I was nuts. Make one wrong move, change some eensy-teensy little thing even if it was only four months in the past, and—who knows?—the Professor might stop work on the Box. I could find myself stuck where I was. For good. And have to repeat the whole four months. But I didn't stop to think out the complications. You could say my brain was still on hold and the excitement of it all had taken over. I mean, *think* of it—walking around in your own past! It was too much to resist. Besides, what was there to worry about if I kept out of my own way? Woody was no problem. Anybody he babbled it to would say he'd been seeing double again.

The sun was shining, there wasn't a cloud in the sky, and it was one of those unusually warm days you get once in a while in December in northern California. More like April than next-door-to-Christmas. A nagging little feeling that not everything was as it should be niggled at me, but I pushed it away. I'd put a good quarter mile between me and the lab building, so what did I have to worry about?

Over in Simmons Square, the little park at the center of campus, the two stands that sold ice cream and hamburgers on weekdays weren't there, but everything else—"Old Main" Hall, Cobb Auditorium, the student union, and Harper Library, one on each side of the square—looked pretty much the same as usual. Except that there were a lot more students around than I had expected for a Saturday. Saturday, December twelfth . . . of course. It was the weekend before exam week. That explained it. They were all either on their way to hole up in Harper Library or were goofing off in desperation. And my luck was holding. I didn't see anybody I recognized.

I bought a hamburger, a couple of doughnuts and a cup of coffee in the student union snack bar and went outside to snag a place at one of the tables under the trees. It was perfectly safe. I never came over to the union for lunch, and with my full-time research work I hadn't had any library reading to do last quarter. If the earlier me *had* come onto campus to do some lab work, I knew for lunch he'd be brown-bagging it out under the trees behind the E. E. building.

Everything's being so ordinary made everything seem more unreal than ever. The sudden thought that the whole thing—Pandora's Box and all—was maybe one big fat hallucination and I had cracked up from working too hard made the last of the second doughnut taste like a damp dog biscuit. A guy with a newspaper was sitting about three tables away, but even squinting like mad I couldn't make out the date on it. There was only my watch to reassure me: it did register the two times, my own 5:33 and twelve minutes to one on the "dual" display. I thought maybe when I finished my coffee, to cheer myself up, I would go over and hang around the Powell Dorm shrubbery on the off chance I might get a glimpse of Polly.

While I was thinking about it, I spotted Professor Poplov tooling across the square on his bike. I shaded my eyes with my hand and kept my coffee cup up in front of my nose until he'd pedaled past, but he never even looked my way. He was wearing that faraway, new-idea-shaping-up frown that meant he wouldn't see Cobb Auditorium unless he ran smack into it.

It was the little kid pedaling after him I should have worried about. I was lowering my coffee cup when he whizzed past, yelling, "Professor Poplov! Hey, Professor!" Maybe he saw me out of the corner of his eye. Anyhow, he swerved, caught his front wheel on the edge of the paved bike path, and went down in a tangle of legs and wheels on the grass. A couple of students ran to help. The rest stopped walking or eating or whatever, and craned to see.

Not me.

I sat there for half a minute feeling like somebody had whanged me between the eyes with a hockey stick.

Then I got up and ran like mad.

The little kid?

He was me.

8

In that awful half minute before I took off from Simmons Square, the old wheels between my ears creaked and groaned and finally started turning, and I saw what a dumb move I'd made, not going back to my own time while I still could. "I never go near Simmons Square at lunchtime"? Hah. But then why should I have remembered pedaling across campus after Professor Poplov that time he dropped his car keys in the parking lot and went rolling off on somebody else's bike?

I'd been silly blind stupid. The fate of Fred the rat—the very *idea* of two Freds—should have been Dire Warning enough for anybody with his head screwed on straight. Seeing another you in the flesh is about as weird as you can get. And as scary.

The scary bit was that only one Fred survived. So what was the obvious question? Can you be in two places at one time, or can't you? O.K., obviously you could. But for how long? Woody never did find out what happened to Fred the Younger. So what besides the fire department cat could it have been? Maybe I read too much sci-fi when I was a kid, but I had a feeling none of the possibilities were cheerful.

* * *

Did I say a little while back I'd had a feeling "something was wrong"? Well, once I'd calmed down a bit, it came to me that it had been more than one something. For a start, my desk top had been weirdly tidy. Thinking back as I ran, I felt like banging my head against the handiest building. Desk top? Hah! That wasn't the half of it. I had looked straight at the Box's Cupboard, and the dime hadn't dropped.

The Box's Cupboard was padlocked.

P-a-d-l-o-c-k-e-d. The push-button electronic lock was gone. Wasn't there yet. And the Imager? Which should have been over against the other wall? It hadn't been there either. How could I have missed missing that? My own project. At that point all my alarm bells should have been ringing for Panic Time. But me? I had waltzed out for a burger and coffee.

I might as well have had my eyes shut, too. Of course the campus looked more like April than December! Maybe it *was* April. It sure wasn't December. Who ever heard of maple trees having nice new green leaves in the winter?

But if I'd gone back further than four months, where —*when* was I?

The answer wasn't hard to find. I slowed to a trot as I passed Oakley Gym and picked up a *Campus Daily* from the stack in the box out in front. And there was the date.

Thursday, April 12, 1984.

Four years back, to the day.

Not months.

Years. The Box had read my MINUS 4 MONTHS as minus four *years*. Which must mean it read only numbers and treated anything following the numbers as garbage. Years, months, days . . . if years were numbers, four months probably should have been something like MINUS 00.04.00. Or just 00:04:00.

You know the feeling you get in some elevators, like you and the elevator are going down faster than your insides are? Well, this felt like somebody'd cut the elevator cable and my stomach had banged up against my Adam's apple.

Four years back I hadn't gone to work for Professor Poplov yet. That desk—that computer terminal—wasn't going to be mine for another year.

So who was Professor Poplov's research assistant four years ago?

You got it.

Max Sharp.

I panicked. About time, too. Next thing I knew, I was sitting on a bench in the garden out behind the history building. I was sunk. Stuck. Doomed. Whatever.

I had left my message for Max the Shark. Where the twelve-year-old me couldn't possibly get at it. My personal entry code for the university computer when I was a freshman was the same one I still had. But I hadn't used it and my own computer-time account to park the message in one of my personal account files where only I—he—could find it. I had left it in a Poplov Labs file. Oh, you'd need my own secret lab-file code to get at it, but so what? That wasn't going to stop the Shark if he came across a mysterious locked file. Once upon a time he hacked his way into the university recorder's triple-coded files just to show the recorder how a computer creep could change his grades from Cs and Ds to As and Bs, and how to fix it so he couldn't. Old Max was good. So I had to figure that he'd stumble onto the file sooner or later, and my dumb message would give him a year or two's head start on his blasted Compat program. So he could get richer and, who knows, maybe dazzle Polly with Jaguars and white suits before she was even out of high school.

I had cut my own throat.

In more ways than one.

The one time in my life I jump off the deep end, and the swimming pool *is* empty. And things could still get worse. I had worried about changing the four months just past. Well, any dumb thing I did now would have four years' time to develop into who-knows-what. Like, Professor Poplov not firing Max. And me never getting to work in Lab C. Or never opening the Box's Cupboard . . .

When I calmed down, I could see that before I did Thing One, I had to get that message out of the university computer. What I needed was a terminal. Fast. There were five or six in Harper Library, but they were right out in the open where any old body could wander up and look over your shoulder. The next nearest place was the Palz Computer Center. I took a couple of classes there my freshman year, so I knew the layout.

I shot off around the corner of the history building like Max the Shark was already breathing down my neck.

It was dead easy. At the Palz Center I kept my thumb over the date on my student I.D. card when I showed it at the reception desk. Then I found a workstation free back in the far corner of the smallest work lab. The twenty or so other students click-clacking away at the keyboards in their little cubicles never even looked up.

Getting into the computer was no sweat. I took a deep breath, entered my computer-time account number, then my access code and then the lab's, and was in. To erase the fatal message, all I had to do was call up the file and *zap*. The next step—the hard part—was figuring out how to get the message to *me*. It had to be now or never. If I got home safe, the Box was going straight back into its cupboard. For good, for all I cared.

O.K. So, I had to get word to me early enough for me to finish Translat before Max came out with Compat, but late enough to cut down the chances of this earlier me doing anything else different than what I had done, and mucking up my past in some unexpected way. But how? I sat and thought for a minute, then tapped out the keyboard command to call up the "real-time clock" from the mainframe's memory. It gives you the month, day, year, hour, minute, and second. For a while I scowled at the digital seconds flicking past. Then all at once—pop!—it was like this big cartoon light bulb switched on over my head. As my granddad used to say, if the answer to How? was a snake, it would've bit me.

All I had to do was write a program that would tie the message to the real-time clock, so that it wouldn't appear in my file until, say, twelve noon on a date, say February twelfth, only two months before the day I had left my own time.

Working out that program took maybe twenty-five minutes. I entered it, took a deep breath, and plunged in.

XS2/3J.0: A WORD TO THE WISE. THE SHARK WILL FINISH WORK ON—

"On what?" growled a strange voice in my ear. "May I see your account card?"

I jumped maybe half a foot. But I was improving. I had my act together by the time I hit the chair seat again, and tapped a fast XOUT to close the file. The screen went blank as I turned to see a security guard shaped like Bluto leaning over me. I felt like Popeye without the can of spinach.

He said it again.

"May I see your computer account card?"

I pulled out my wallet and fished the card out from behind my student ID card, and handed it over meekly. He fished one just like it out of his shirt pocket and held the two up together.

I almost stopped breathing. The other one was newish, and mine, even laminated in plastic, was pretty beat-up—but looking at them from the back, I could see the squiggle of thread that I'd laminated in. The identical same squiggle in both.

It wasn't hard to guess what must have happened. Somehow the other me—from here on I'd better call him Jacko (which is what my folks called me back then), or this will get more confusing than it is already—anyhow, he'd tracked me down. But why? And how, when I last saw him flat on his face? Unless he'd gone off and settled down to work at a terminal somewhere—maybe even here in the center—and found that somebody else was accessing the Poplov Labs files.

The guard was still scowling like he was afraid I was some Mad Hacker about to sabotage the whole computer system. "I think you better come out with me to the office, Mister, uh, Russell, and see if we can clear this up."

Jacko had to be in the office. I knew it.

I was scared spitless. First, I could see me getting tangled up with all sorts of complications and never making it back to the E. E. lab building for my twelve-hour deadline. And then . . . meet myself? No, thanks! Who knows what might happen? Shake hands, and *phhht*, one of me is gone? Both, maybe. Like matter and antimatter. O.K., so I wasn't making any sense. What else was new?

"This way," Bluto said when we got to the door.

But I turned left, fast, when he turned right. Down past the tutorial office, I ducked in through the director's secretary's empty office, out the French doors onto the back patio, and over the wall. The secretary came back in from the director's office as I was rolling over the wall, but for once I was lucky. She sat down at her desk without giving a look my way.

I whizzed around to the front of the building, figuring

Bluto would have headed for the back entrance—and there was my old bike propped up against the railings. So the other—so Jacko *had* tracked me down.

The bike wasn't locked. Philosophical quibbles aside, I figured it was as much mine as his, so I hopped on and pedaled off toward University Boulevard like I had a posse on my tail. The sooner I got off campus the better. What I needed was somewhere to sit down and pull myself together. To figure what to do next. I looked over my shoulder once. Jacko-Me was a couple hundred yards behind, pumping along like mad. It hadn't taken him long to find a bike to borrow—I knew me well enough to know he hadn't pinched it. Maybe he borrowed it from Bluto.

"Hey, you!" he called after me. "Wait a minute!"

I pushed harder still, and pulled on ahead, but it wasn't easy with the bicycle seat five awkward inches too low. The four years' muscle I had on him was all that saved me, because the little guy wasn't going to call it quits. When, face red and jaw clenched, he came whizzing up out of the underpass where Thompson Boulevard dips under Lake Avenue and the railway, our bike and I were tucked up in the shrubbery on the embankment, looking down at him. At me. He sure was determined. Not even the downtown traffic or craning to see if I'd turned down a side street slowed him up much. Way down at Shelford Street he hung a right, which meant he was going home before heading back to campus to return the bike.

Once I untangled my own from the shrubbery, I rode off in the other direction. I played it safe, taking the long way around campus to Peterson Park up in the foothills, and spent the rest of the afternoon sitting under a tree in a fit of the glums. I didn't know what to do next. For the first time in my life, I didn't know what to do. The old brain-box had crashed. Shut down. What I did see was that I had asked for everything I got. Jump off a cliff, and you can't exactly complain when you go splat. What ever happened to my almost lifelong practice at being cool, calm, and cautious? *Splat.*

At least I still had—*hoped* I had—my emergency parachute. When my twelve hours were up, I could go back when I'd come from. Maybe Jacko had blown my chance to warn him about Max. Maybe I didn't dare try climbing in my bedroom window and using my old computer to try hacking into the university mainframe, for fear of landing in an even worse mess. At least, if I could keep from putting my foot in it until half past midnight, I could get *home.*

Home. But without having tossed a wrench in Max's works.

And with no prospect of winning Polly back.

I felt like banging my head against the tree. Actually, I did, but once was enough. For a gesture of frustration, I do not recommend it. You get more ringing in the ears than relief. Besides, with Polly so much on my mind, I figured my brains were scrambled enough already.

By seven o'clock the sun had slid behind the hills, the air had turned chilly, and I was as miserable as I was hungry. Otherwise I would never have talked myself into grabbing a bite to eat somewhere in town. Or, as soon as it was dark, into riding over to Melville Street and climbing the old maple tree in the Armbrusters' side garden to see if I could catch a look at Polly at her fourteenth-birthday party. Not only was April twelfth Polly's birthday, but this one was *the* birthday. The one when I got invited to her party for the first time ever, and popped the great would-you-like-to-go-to-the-movies-Saturday? question. O.K., so I was feeling pretty mushy and sorry for myself, but could *you* resist the chance to eavesdrop on the happiest minute of your life? I figured it was safe enough. Most of that evening I—sorry—Jacko would have his eyes glued to Polly.

This time, with less than six hours to go before I had to be back in Poplov Lab C, I told myself I wasn't taking any chances. I even sorted out the bills in my wallet and the change in my pocket. If I got hauled off to the police station for trying to pay for a meal with a five-dollar bill dated four years in the future, the custard would really hit the fan.

I coasted down Peterson Hill onto campus, parked the bike against the railing beside the back door of the E. E. building, walked down into town, and had a pizza at Toto's because it was the only pizza place in town I'd never eaten in. I still had a lot to learn. Tinker with time, and *any*thing can be a disaster. Or a close call. I was halfway through a Toto's Special with everything, when in comes Gavin Kott, this old friend of my big brother Phil's, with his wife and their two kids. He gives me this funny look, and suddenly my mouthful of pizza tastes like mozzarella-flavored library paste. When I swallowed, it felt like a golf ball going down.

Why was he staring? Nobody in his right mind would take me for shrimpy Jacko Russell.

But what about big Phil Russell?

That had to be it. Any minute, he was going to come over and ask if I was related to Phil. I could tell from the way he leaned over and said something to his wife and she slid a look at me and then nodded. So I jumped up, snagged the waitress, and asked if I could take the rest of my pizza in a doggy bag. She brought it to me over at the cash register while I was paying the bill.

Close call or no, it wasn't enough to shoo the biggest bee out of my bonnet. I still had it in my head to stake out Polly's birthday party and wallow in a little self-pity. It was already pretty dark outside, so I walked on over the six blocks to the alley that runs along behind Melville Street. And nearly ended up with cardiac arrest out by our garage when my dad opened the gate in the high fence, switched on the light above the garage door, and headed for the garbage cans with a bulging plastic bag. If I'd flattened myself any flatter into the shadows along my stretch of fence, you'd have had to peel me off, cartoon-style. As soon as the light blinked out and the gate banged shut, I was off again. Next door at the Armbrusters, I went in over the hedge beside the garage.

Through the window in the back door I could see Mrs. Armbruster and Adelle, her once-a-week maid, busy in the brightly lit kitchen. The side garden over by the big old maple tree—which was where I was heading—

was dark. The light from the house didn't reach that far. I edged over to and then along the fence that ran between the Armbrusters' and our house. Once I reached the maple tree, I hung my blazer over a handy branch, and then swung myself up onto another one. Like old times.

Polly's party had reached the cake and ice-cream stage. Kenny Ross, Joe Vogle, and Robbie Potter were sitting out on the front steps, feeding their faces with cake. Robbie had a plate on each knee. And there I was in my tree with a front-row balcony seat for the living room, kitchen, upstairs, hall, and Polly's room. The living-room windows were shut so the music wouldn't bother Mrs. Mott across the street—I remembered that—but the kitchen and some of the upstairs ones were open. Every once in a while, usually when the record on the hi-fi was being changed, I could hear Mrs. Armbruster telling Adelle to take more fruit punch or brownies or whatever into the dining room table. It was a while before I spotted Polly. I didn't see me at all. Jacko, I mean.

(Look, I have *got* to stop talking about him as "me," or you'll never be able to keep us straight, and I'll keep getting knotted up about how it felt—about being both me and somebody apart from me, I mean. So he's Jacko, period, from here on in. O.K.? O.K.)

Where was I? Oh, yeah. Polly. She came through the dining room with Jimmy Gardiner and Roger Mussey trailing after her like a couple of cocker spaniels. After a while she was gone again, and it was maybe five minutes before her bedroom light went on and she came flouncing in with Shirley Hart in tow and slammed the door behind them. And shrieked and stamped her foot.

"Where *is* that little twerp?" I heard her say. She snatched a pillow off the bed and slung it at the door. "He was supposed to be here at *six-thirty!*"

Eavesdropping may be immoral—sneaky, anyhow—but you couldn't have pried me out of that tree at any price. There was Shirl, flapping her hands and looking over her shoulder all the time like the conspirator in an old silent movie who's afraid someone's listening at the door. And Polly! This was a new Polly to me. All I had ever seen was the cute little blond kitty-cat. This one was more cute little tiger cat. I decided I sort of liked that. I wondered who had got her so steamed up.

"I hate him!" she squealed.

I guess Shirl was trying to get her to shut up, because after Polly raged around the room a couple more times, I heard her groan and say, "Oh, O.K.! But you have to stay by the front door and tell me the *minute* he gets here."

After that they went downstairs. With my view through the living room into the hall, I saw Polly go into the dining room beyond, come back out with two plates with big pieces of cake, and head back along the hall toward the kitchen. I didn't see Shirley. I guess she had orders to sit down on the stairs so she could watch the front door for the missing twerp.

I figured Polly was taking her mom and Adelle a piece of her big fancy cake—I remembered it being three tiers high, with pink-icing roses all over—but through the kitchen window I saw her sail right past them and out the back door.

There was just enough light from the window in the kitchen door for me to see that somebody was sitting out there on the back porch. Somebody who got more than a piece of cake. After Polly sat down beside him on the bench, she leaned over and gave him a shy little peck on the cheek.

I nearly fell out of the tree. *Jacko*?

It must be. I hadn't seen him anywhere else. But for Pete's sake, how—

"Hey, you!"

The unexpected voice at my back was so close I lost my balance and had to grab for the tree trunk.

"You in the tree. What are you doing out there?"

I turned around to peer through the dark leaves behind me, and there was Jacko, leaning out of my bedroom window.

9

Our bedroom window, that is.

"I warn you," he said stiffly. "Identify yourself at once or I'll—I shall summon the police."

You would think, in a crisis like this, all I could have thought of was (a) putting the tree trunk between me and him so he wouldn't see who I was, (b) getting the heck out of there, (c) how my heart was breaking into little bits as I realized that if Jacko wasn't at the party next door, then he wasn't on the Armbrusters' back porch. And that Polly was a two-faced little flirt. The twerp she had ordered Shirley to watch out for must be —had to be—me. Him. Jacko. All three thoughts did flit through my mind, but mostly I was wondering, *Is that what I sound like?* Like, as Professor Poplov had put it, a snooty butler in some old movie? I had worked hard ever since I was ten and in the tenth grade to polish up my vocabulary and sound—well, older. Sophisticated. Hearing it from Jacko, I had a sneaking suspicion that maybe it sounded more like stuffed twerp.

"Speak up!" he ordered, with a faint, unsophisticated squeak to his voice. "I need only one hand for the telephone. It's a push-button model. With the other I have you covered. I warn you, I'm an excellent shot."

The way he was holding it, silhouetted against the

bedroom light, a very near-sighted burglar might have thought the thing was a gun, but I saw it was my old Australian "hummingbird" boomerang—and nothing to laugh at. Back when I was in practice, I was so good with it that I used it to bring down the apples in our apple tree that were too high up to reach from the ladder. My dad called me Deadeye Jack. Maple leaves or no, Deadeye Jack might still whang me in the eye.

Since I couldn't let him see me, I chose possibility (a), scrambling around to the far side of the trunk to put it between him and me. From there, with (b) in mind, I eased down to the next big branch.

"Hey, you! Stop!"

Swinging down from the lower branch, I dropped the ten or so feet to the ground, scared spitless I would land on a tree root in the dark and break an ankle. But I didn't, and I would have got away clear if, just as I was streaking for the street, old Jacko hadn't shone my big old camping lantern out the window after me. Later, I figured it was the white shirt that gave me away.

Every move I made seemed to backfire, I thought as I loped down Melville Street. At least the both of me were still around and in good health. Neither of us had gone *pop!* and Vanished Forever. Some consolation. I was still a walking disaster area. One little accident—Jacko's finding out I was accessing that computer file—had probably ruined my whole life. And whose fault was that? If he got home too late to get dressed up for the party, it was probably because of trying to track me down, maybe having to return the borrowed bike, having to walk home—who knows what else? So, he hadn't had a chance to ask Polly to the movies. So, they wouldn't go on Saturday. And he wouldn't buy her a double-fudge banana split supremo at the Dairy Dell afterward. And . . . so on and so on. Now he might never get up the nerve to ask her. She might never forgive him for not having shown up. Face it, I told myself. Your romance is a nonevent.

That stopped me dead right in the middle of crossing Parker Street, and it was only thanks to the good brakes and loud horn on the BMW that almost ran me down that you are hearing this story.

The question was, I said to myself as I reached the opposite sidewalk and trotted on, after what I'd seen and heard from the maple tree, did I really *want* Jacko to ask her to the movies? The mere thought that Polly might have been stringing me along for four years because I could afford fancy birthday presents and because the senior class had voted me most likely to be the class's first millionaire, made me shrivel. Dumb, dumb, *twerp*! Still . . .

I didn't hear the bike coming whispering up behind me. First thing I know, this familiar voice is saying, "Is this by any chance your blazer?"

And there he was. Jacko again. Pedaling along at my elbow, holding out the jacket I had left hanging on the Armbrusters' maple tree. He hadn't returned the bike yet after all.

"Look, I'm sorry I alarmed you," he said, panting a little. "I only . . ."

But I didn't care what he only. I grabbed the blazer

and took off like Roadrunner. Jacko might be on wheels, but we were only a block from the railroad tracks, and I knew where there was a break in the chain-link fence. I hadn't tried in a couple of years, but figured I could probably still squeeze through. There was no way he could get the bike through, and he wouldn't catch me without it. By the time he went around by the Thompson Boulevard underpass, I would be long gone.

I made it across the tracks, out through the train station, and up into the tangle of tree-lined streets west of campus in no time flat. When I got to the little park beside the day-care center, I flopped down on a bench back in the shadows away from the streetlight to catch my breath.

I pushed the little button that lit up the face of my watch. Twelve minutes past nine. More than three hours left until Pandora switched on again. Plenty of time to face up to the Polly Problem.

The suspicion that I had been Polly's pet cocker spaniel for four years had me feeling pretty seasick. How could I have thought that beautiful Apollonia Armbruster could really have liked a shrimpy little twelve year old? But how could I tell Jacko? He would not only not pop the Saturday-matinee question, he would run the other way when he saw her coming.

And that . . .

And that would mean that four years from today I wouldn't be taking Polly out to lunch at the Gilded Shrimp. Or, for that matter, seeing her drive off with Max Sharp.

Or finding and using the Box.

I knew the line out of *The Riddle of Time* by heart: "Backward time travelers would have to be aware before they left Point A (present time) for Point B (past time) that they must by some means arrive back at A—the original time, at the original place—or they *will never have been there to go back in the first place.*"

In which case, *Phhht!* And even if *The Riddle of Time* was wrong, I was in trouble. Change the past that little bit too much, and I could be stuck where—or rather, "when"—I was.

Two hours later I was still trying to wrap my mind around this nasty little detail, and getting nowhere. Forget about ending up rich and famous enough to make Polly go weak at the knees. Survival was Problem Number One.

Survival. For starters you need your wits about you. Most of mine were still on vacation, and the rest were scurrying nowhere, like the pet gerbil I once had, on his little exercise treadmill. Just to give you a sample: say I got into Lab C in time to climb back through the Box's time window. O.K.? Now, the easy assumption is that I am then back where I started from. Right? Not necessarily. Already, I figure, I have put my foot in it so efficiently in this past time that what *I* call "my past" may be changed beyond repair. In which case, now that he's missed Polly's party, in lots of little ways Jacko will probably keep on *not* doing what I did in those four years. And who knows where he might be four years on? So. So what happens to *me*-me when I put my foot through the time window and he's not waiting on the other side? And even if he is, what then? So we join up, so to speak. Sure, Jacko is me, but what happens to *my* memories of those four in-between years?

Phhht?

Still, there wasn't any help for it. I had to go back to the lab and take another blind jump off the high dive.

At half past eleven I made my way back toward the west campus and tucked myself into the shadows under the big redwood tree opposite the front entrance of the Poplov Labs. The campus cops would be driving past pretty soon on their regular patrol route. I would wait until a quarter past midnight, then let myself in at the front—no, at the loading dock door. You couldn't see that one from the street. I ought to be inside Lab C in under five minutes. That left less than ten minutes to wait before the Box reopened the time window.

I heard the cop car coming a good while before it finally crawled past, flicking its spotlight over the lab building windows and doors, and then over the Plant Research Institute's equipment sheds across the street. When the coast was clear, I zipped around the corner of the lab building and made my way along the rear, where there was just the one security light. (One was enough, because the only windows on that side are at least twenty feet up and protected with steel mesh.) I meant to creep past like your standard silent prowler, but no such luck. It was noisy going, with all those eucalyptus berries crunching underfoot, and I sounded like three or four of me.

As it turned out, there were only two.

Plus two bicycle wheels.

You guessed it. The human suction cup had caught up with me again.

He was out of breath. "Where did you go?" he panted. "I've searched up and down every street between here and the railroad twice, and all over campus. I'm really sorry I threatened to boomerang you. Why didn't you just say who you were?"

All this time I was backing off, you understand. Not really because I thought one of us might go *pop!* but because it felt so weird. I mean, there *I* was, not three feet away from me.

"Who—who I am?" I asked faintly.

"Your name's Russell, isn't it? I observed the name tape in your blazer."

I hadn't known my name was *in* the new jacket yet, or I never would have taken it off. Leave it to my mom the name-tape freak! Would you believe, when I went away to camp she even put them in my socks? I used to have J. Russell stitched all over me.

"Ye-es," I said weakly, trying to think what besides John and James began with J. "Joe. Joe Russell. Why do you want to know? No, don't tell me. Look, I would appreciate it if you would just pedal off home and leave me alone. Please!"

I knew I was wasting my breath. He had this squinty-eyed, happy-intense look I get when I'm on the track of some new idea. But then he surprised me.

"Don't you get—I mean, don't you understand?" he

asked excitedly. "That explains why they confused our computer accounts. My name is Russell too. John Russell. We must be cousins. You look too much like the old photographs of my brother Phil in his high-school yearbook for us not to be." He held out his hand. "I'm delighted to make your acquaintance, Joe."

This formal touch while I am skulking in the shrubbery, planning to break into a top-secret lab, was too much. I almost snapped out, "The delight, I regret, is not mutual," but figured he would think I was making fun of the way he talked. I tried to think how Max the Shark might put it.

"Look, kiddo, this is all very interesting," I whispered, "but call back tomorrow. I'm busy, you're in the way, and you ought to be tucked up in beddy-bye. So buzz off."

By this time we had got as far as the end of the labs, so I took a quick look around the corner toward the loading dock, and ducked back again.

"You still here?" I looked at my watch. Ten minutes to midnight.

He was standing there looking hurt. And who knows? Maybe he would have taken off. But right then (and I had thought things couldn't get any worse!) there was this deep rumble and hiss of air brakes from around the far side of the building. Like a bus or maybe a trailer truck had pulled into the parking lot.

I guess I must have looked kind of wild-eyed at that point, because old Jacko gave me this smug little smile as he carefully propped the bike against the wall. "I believe I will stay, thank you, Joe. Just to be sure that you're not contemplating some illegality."

"Oh, shut up!" I hissed. Come *on*. I was never that pompous. Was I? Anyhow, what could I do but ignore him? I crept around the corner and up into the pine trees on the hillside at the back of the building. The pine needles were silent underfoot, and I moved quickly. Jacko stuck so close that twice he stepped on my heel and I almost walked out of my shoe. I gave him what I hoped was a shriveling glare, and I guess it did dampen him down a little because he blinked a couple of times and then swallowed hard.

"I have to stay," he whispered the next time I stopped. I could hardly hear him. "I'm afraid to go home by myself. It's spooky going through the railroad underpass. There was this man sitting down there on the walkway, yelling things."

What could I say to that? For one thing, it was the first time he'd sounded like a genuine kid. But what on earth was I going to *do* with him?

I didn't have an answer, and a moment later I had forgotten the question. Don't let anybody ever tell you that life can't get any more complicated than it is already. It can. And it did. By this time we were right above the loading dock, which is at the east side of the back end of the building, and from where we stood we could see most of the parking lot beyond.

Including the power company cherry picker that, with a gentle whine, was lifting its passenger bucket up to one of the topmost windows of Lab C.

10

"*That*'s your appointment? That power company truck?" Jacko sounded as if he'd expected something like Madonna in a trenchcoat and dark glasses, and I had let him down.

He also sounded loud. I grabbed him quick and clapped my hand over his mouth.

"Mm-ugm-mgh!" He wriggled like a fish, but I held on.

"I'll let go, but you'll have to keep quiet," I whispered.

"Mm-mgh!"

With that, he bit my hand—hard—and followed up with a mean kick to the shin. I was so surprised, I almost let go. Instead, I lost my balance and the two of us went over backward onto the pine needles, me still holding on. Thanks to the pine needles it was a quiet crash, and with the soft whine of the cherry picker raising its bucket, I hoped maybe the men below hadn't heard us.

I guess it knocked some of the starch out of me for a minute as well as the wind, because what I wheezed in Jacko's ear was, "Cut it out, pea brain. Those guys aren't power company. If they were, they wouldn't need a cherry picker. All the power lines on campus are underground."

Until I said that, I hadn't remembered the stolen

power company truck that had been seen barreling on up the street after the labs' alarm went off last (so to speak) night. The one the cops found abandoned the next day out by the freeway. If these were the same guys, this was serious.

The kid stopped wriggling and made signs—ending up with crossing his heart—to show he was going to keep quiet. When I let go, even in the shadowy darkness under the trees, I could see his eyes wide and shining with excitement.

"You mean they're after something in Professor Poplov's lab?"

"Possibly," I whispered back.

I looked at my watch. 12:03. I was torn between wanting to know what the heck the fake repairmen were up to, and wishing they'd hurry up and get whatever it was over with. I *had* to be inside Lab C in fifteen minutes. Twenty at the latest. Any later than that and—if the Box's time window materialized at all—I would be lucky to catch the train as it pulled out of the station, as you might say.

"Look!" Jacko whispered. He raised up and peered down the slope. "You're right—they're wearing ski masks! Who are they? Spies? Industrial espionage agents?"

I didn't have an inkling, so I just shook my head and tried to look mysterious. He nodded, suddenly serious. Maybe he thought I meant the answer was classified and he didn't have security clearance.

Actually, lying on the ground we had a better view

down through the trees than the one we'd had standing up—no branches in the way, and a clear view down between the tree trunks to the parking lot below. The guy riding the cherry picker bucket must have unscrewed one of the security lights because the lot was dimmer than it had been, but I could still see the bucket where it had stopped at the cornermost of the top range of windows, one high above the spare-equipment lockup at the back end of Lab C, and the closest corner to us. They couldn't have been more than sixty feet away.

"Do you work for the government?" Jacko whispered.

Looking over, in the faint glimmer of light from below I could make out the kid looking at me the way I guess I must have looked at my brother Phil back when he made the Winter Olympics bobsled team. It felt really weird.

"No. The university," I said uncomfortably. That was perfectly true, even if not in the way he meant. "Will you kindly just shut up and watch? I want to listen."

He shut up.

I could see the guy in the bucket groping around along the corrugated wall just above the corner windows. It looked as if they weren't trying to break into the lab after all. He seemed to be searching for something. When he found whatever it was, he made a sharp, tugging motion and, unfastening a shiny object from his belt, fumbled with it for a while. It must have been something like a fishing reel, because after that he began motions that looked like pulling, then reeling in, pulling and reeling in.

Pulling and reeling in. A wire. He was reeling in a wire. A wire that must have been threaded through the window frame . . .

"Wow!" Jacko breathed in my ear. "I'll bet it's a bug—a concealed microphone, I mean. Is that your assessment of the situation?"

I wasn't so sure. "Maybe. If it is, wires are out of date. That could be why they're getting rid of it. By now they could have a wafer transmitter smaller than the size of a penny. And for—" I broke off impatiently. *Assessment of the situation?* He sounded like even his underwear was starched. It was beginning to set my teeth on edge. I tried to tell myself it was only because it didn't go with his jeans and track shoes and being a kid. *I* didn't sound that bad.

Forget it, I thought. Keep your eye on the ball (or words to that effect). I focused on the guy on lookout out by the parking-area entrance, and tried to work out whether he could see the front door from where he stood. Now, if I could sneak back around . . .

That's when Jacko gave me a mean elbow in the ribs. Otherwise I would have missed seeing the guy in the bucket reach up to raise a corner of one of the corrugated roof panels and lift out a black box the size of a small shoebox. Once he had it out, he fiddled with it for a minute as if he was unfastening something (another wire?), stowed it in the bucket and replaced it with a second box half the size, then shoved the roof panel back into place and signaled the man below, who headed back for the truck.

"Curiouser and curiouser," Jacko quoted in a whisper.

I hadn't thought about *Alice in Wonderland* or *Through the Looking Glass* since I was a kid, but they sure fit the way I'd felt since noon. Stepping through into a world where everything you do backfires . . . I took a quick look at my watch. 12:18. When I saw that, I got really wound up. Bugs, wires, black boxes? Who cared? All I wanted was to get back through my looking glass.

"They're going! Is that all?" Jacko sounded disappointed. "What should we do? Call the cops? Or tail them? You can use the bike if you want."

They had moved really fast. The bucket shifted sideways along the wall to the dead security light, the light sprang on, the bucket whined down, and the man in it jumped out and into the cab beside the driver. They took off out of the lot and up the street with a loud squeal of rubber.

Jacko watched while I fumbled my key into the lock of the door next to the loading dock. "Hey, you really *do* work for the university!"

"Umh."

"*Are* you going to call the cops?"

"Uh. Leave it to me," I evaded.

The key turned stiffly.

"I'll come in with you."

"Oh, no, you won't. You stay right where you are, and keep out of sight. I'll phone your father to come out and pick you up." I didn't have much time left—only nine minutes—but I owed him that.

"But—"

"No buts." I slipped inside and tried to shut the door on him, but the twerp was too fast for me. He stuck so close that about all that *didn't* get through was the proverbial foot.

"Ow! My foot!"

"Get out of here!" I was frantic. "You'll ruin everything."

But once he got his foot free, he wouldn't budge. And I didn't have time to argue. I'll leave him in the hall, I thought. He wasn't going to get past me twice. I locked the door behind us and felt my way through the storerooms and into the windowless back hall. I found the light switch, flicked it on, drew a mental bead on the Lab A door, switched the light off again, and made for the door in the dark. Jacko was right at my heels, talking a blue streak the whole time.

"It looked to me as if he must have been replacing or upgrading a surveillance system. What do you think? I'd like a look at those black boxes. How long do you suppose the old one was up there? Professor Poplov told us after Fourier optics class this morning that he was starting work on something new. You don't suppose they could have tapped right into his computer keyboard, do you?"

They could have. And how long *had* the box and wire been up there? I was getting some funny ideas, but my watch said 12:25 and I didn't have time to have funny ideas, like remembering Professor Poplov always grumbled that the guy who patented the K-laser had pirated his hyperlaser design, only he didn't know how. He said the K-laser was why he switched to electronic locks.

So the pirates had already done that piece of dirty work. Because at the very minute I was punching in the code for the Lab A door, and if the locks came after the fact . . .

But there was no time left to worry about all that.

I switched on the lights and broke into Jacko's rush of questions. "This is as far as you go," I said. I pointed at the phone beside the drawing table. "You call your dad yourself, and let yourself out the way we came in." I pulled the loading-dock door key off my ring and tossed it to him.

His hand reached out automatically, but the key clattered to the floor, and he gaped at me, goggle-eyed with alarm.

I'd forgotten he hadn't seen me really close up and in a good light before. So? I didn't look *that* much like Phil used to, did I?

It was worse than that.

"You've got a scar on your chin just like mine," he accused in a voice that had gone all squeaky. "And—and the same double mole over by your ear. Who—who *are* you? You're not an investigator at all. You haven't even called the police. Why do you want to get into Professor Poplov's private lab in the middle of the night?"

I backed up against the Lab B door, ready to zip in and slam the door after me as soon as I'd entered the combination on the lock panel. But how the heck was

I supposed to hold him off, tap out the numbers, and keep him from seeing what they were? I held up both hands and waggled them the way you do when you're trying to calm somebody down.

"Trust me." I tried hard to sound cool and calm. "Just call Dad and get out of here. If you get caught inside the building, you'll *never* get to work for Professor Poplov."

Even before I knew what it was, I knew I'd said something wrong. The kid's eyes went so wide you could see the whites all the way around.

"*Dad*? You said 'Dad.' Like h-he was yours too. And there are—" He was a sort of greeny pale, but he came closer. "There are five little scars on your hands. Like m-mine."

I think I turned greeny pale myself. The scars on my palm were from falling on the garden rake the time I invented a garbage-bag parachute when I was four and jumped off the garage roof. The chute had worked, but I hadn't allowed for side-slip.

"There's a machine in there, isn't there?" Jacko whispered. He stared past me to the inner lab door. "A time machine. It wasn't a joke. All Professor Poplov's kidding around about time machines wasn't a joke, was it? There really is one. And you . . ."

He swallowed hard.

"You—you're *me*."

11

"Holy *moley*!"

Jacko stared across Lab C at the Box's "window." Its large, bright patch hovered in the darkness a foot and a half above floor level.

"Why is it so light?"

"It was about a quarter past five in the afternoon when I left. It's probably not much more than that now. As soon as the Box completed its transmit period, it would compute the time adjustment and switch to the recall command."

Nervously, Jacko moved closer to peer into it.

"There is! There's a kind of platform in there. And all you have to do is step up on it, and you're gone? It looks like it's just hanging in midair."

I looked at my watch for maybe the ninety-eighth time. I groaned. "Three more minutes and seventeen seconds and it won't be. Not that it really matters. Everything's changed. There won't be the same 'then' for me to get to. When I get there I'll be you. I mean, *I* won't be me. You will. Oh, garbage! I don't know what I mean." I glared at him in despair. "If *only* you hadn't skipped Apollonia Armbruster's party."

Jacko flapped an impatient hand. "Why worry about

Polly Armbruster's party when there's all—all *this*? Besides, what does she have to do with it?" Funny. He seemed to have forgotten all his six-syllable words.

"Nothing. Absolutely nothing. Only that you were going to invite her to the movies and she was going to say yes, and we've been going to the movies every Saturday ever since."

The rest of it, for some reason—I wasn't exactly sure why—felt too embarrassing to explain. Not so much the part about Pandora's Cupboard and Polly being the reason for my opening it, but about Max the Shark and the Jaguar and me wanting to be rich so I could get Polly everything she wanted. I still sort of wanted that. But it was—well—

"Honest?" Jacko beamed. "I thought maybe Polly was sort of hinting around about going to see *Splash!* this Saturday, but I wasn't sure. *I* know I'm older than my age, but I was worried it might not show. Gosh! If you know she's going to say yes, what's the problem? I can go over to her house after supper tomorrow and ask her then."

"No!" I blurted. I was so rattled I surprised me as well as him. But then—after all, why not? It might be the answer. But there wasn't time to untangle it all. I had a high dive to jump off of.

"Besides—" Jacko had this puzzled look, as if I must have mislaid half my marbles, "why shouldn't your own 'then' be there for you to get to? Nothing in between now and then has changed *yet*."

I blinked. I had the feeling it couldn't be as simple as that, but it sounded logical. I felt a bit better. There might be a foot or two of water in the swimming pool after all.

Twenty-seven seconds.

I almost hated to go. Almost. But then again, I couldn't wait to get out of there.

"Be sure all the doors are locked behind you," I warned. I knew—who better?—that he wanted to work with Professor Poplov so badly that he'd keep his mouth shut about our break-in.

With less than twenty seconds left, I stuck my hand in the light, felt the platform, and climbed through.

And? And there I was. Standing at the edge of the projection-field platform. With the Box's twelve klaser beams still humming away. All of three seconds later, they shut down. Talk about close calls! Any closer and I might have left the seat of my pants behind.

It was funny—all that last hour I'd been jumpy as a frog on a hot skillet, but I hadn't been what I'd call scared. Now my knees were wobbling so wildly that I barely made it over to a lab stool to sit down and catch my breath. I was back! I rubbed my eyes—things were a little bit out of focus—but I could read the wall clock. It said 5:34.

I had been gone twelve hours and it had taken less than twenty minutes.

And then I heard this noise. Like someone behind me drawing a long, deep breath. I spun the stool around.

Someone behind me *was* taking a long, deep breath. Jacko.

* * *

He was standing in the middle of the projection-field platform. Staring at the Box.

"Wow!"

"How—how—" I couldn't even get the question out, I was so startled. And scared.

"I was right behind you."

"But you can't *be* here. You've got to get out. You've got to go back. Think of Mom and Dad," I babbled, heading for the Box. "Don't move. I'm sending you right back."

But already he had jumped down and was circling the Imager where it stood on the far side of the platform from the Box.

"You've *got* to go back!"

I must have yelled pretty loud, because he jumped. "Look, if you get stuck here," I pleaded, "there's no J. J. Russell at *all* four years ago. If there's no four-years-ago me, how can there be a here-and-now me? I'll—I'll—evaporate!"

I looked around wildly. It was like I was fading already. My guess now is maybe I imagined it—lose your head and you can convince yourself of almost anything—but I was sure I could see this faint shadow of everything in Lab B right through the Lab C wall. I tell you, it was *weird*. But panicky or no, I managed to get the Box switched on and booted up the EDWFR program. Jacko edged close enough to watch, but he was careful to keep out of reach. In case I tried to jump him, I guess.

"If you'll only listen," he protested when I stopped jabbering, "I *will* go. All you have to do is program this thing so both of us can go—"

"Both of us?" I squeaked. "No way."

"Will you just listen? So both of us can go back to last summer—last summer for me, I mean—before that research lab in Maryland beat Professor Poplov out with the K-laser just like the hyperlaser he was working on. Don't you get it? If we can warn him about the bug and the black box, the cops will catch the crooks and the Poplov Labs won't have anything left to worry about."

It was just the kind of Noble Idea a kid *would* come up with. But, you know, it wasn't half bad. And what if there wasn't only Professor Poplov's hyperlaser? What about poor old Woody, with both ten years' work and his girl down the drain? What if he'd been pirated too?

"Afterward," Jacko explained eagerly, "we come back here. You send me home in time to go to Apoll—Polly's birthday party. And I ask her to the movies. What do you say?"

What could I say? I know: no way could it be that easy. But any chance to get back to Square One . . . besides, I had it in my head there wasn't time to argue. As Jacko moved off toward the platform, I could have sworn I saw the shapes of the equipment he walked past all the time he was walking past. Like, through him. O.K., just dimly. And O.K., maybe I was hysterical. But when in doubt, get a move on.

As fast as I could, I programmed the Box for another ten-minute transmission, not five years back as Jacko had suggested, but to noon on April twelfth *eight* years ago, with one ten-minute recall set for three hours later—you could get into too much trouble in twelve—and one more nine hours after that, in case we got into trouble anyhow. I was all set to enter the command to run the program when this little alarm bell went off in the back of my head. What if eight April twelfths ago landed us on a weekday? With lab assistants around to walk in on us. I screwed my eyes shut and did a little fast calculation. No, it was O.K. Eight years ago April twelfth had been a Saturday. Saturday. That had been the day of . . . forget it, I told myself. This was no time for nostalgia.

I held my breath until the Box started to hum, and then made for the platform. It was maybe twenty seconds before the faint, bright patch of air appeared, and as soon as I could see the concrete floor down through it, I shoved Jacko up and jumped up after him. I think my last thought was "What am I *doing*?"

Jacko—very funny—yelled, "Way to go-o-o-o!"

Lab C didn't look much like its old—its future self. The ceiling, the girders that supported it, and the catwalks were all still—no, cross that out—they were already painted a pale pukey green. The big windows along the east wall were clear glass, with wide strips of butcher paper taped over the panes of the lower half. I was used to seeing the frosted-bathroom-window kind of glass there, with wire mesh inside the glass. Up across the far end of the room, behind the machinery that runs the overhead crane for shifting heavy equipment, there was a long workbench instead of the storage lockers. Five or six big wooden crates addressed to Poplov, E. E. Dept., had been shoved underneath it, and the new equipment they had contained sat around in a drift of packing litter.

Half a dozen ordinary steel gym-style lockers were lined up beside the door to Lab B, and the cupboards and worktables under the wall clock were a collection of old, beat-up odds and ends.

Only the wall clock looked familiar. It said 12:01, just what it was supposed to say. Good old Box. Who knows what I did wrong the first time!

Good old Jacko looked a little pale around the gills as he moved away from the shadowy patch that was the Box's time window.

"W-what went wrong?" he wavered. "This can't be last summer. It's too d-different."

"Don't agitate y—don't get yourself in a sweat," I amended. "We've gone back eight years. Why do things halfway? I'm pretty sure that Professor Poplov's hyper-laser wasn't the first project developed here that some-body else got the credit for. Do you know Woody New-burger yet?"

"No. Who's Woody Newburger?"

"You've seen a tall, skinny lab assistant who goes around with a rat in his pocket, haven't you?"

Jacko nodded.

"Uh, yes. Well, what we're in ought to be 1980. *Is* 1980. Right now Woody is the Professor's chief research assistant. In a couple of months he should be submitting the dissertation on his research project so he can get his doctor's degree. But two weeks or so before his deadline, somebody in Rhode Island is going to publish the same work and walk off with a juicy electronics contract."

Not that I am slow on the uptake or anything. But—

would you believe?—it wasn't until I heard that last sentence come out of my mouth that it occurred to me to wonder about Maxwell Sharp III and his marvelous Compat chip.

The Shark? But he was rich already. At least, his dad was.

Sheer coincidence.

Had to be.

"I get it!" Jacko grinned happily. "You think the pirates' black box is planted up there already, and it's snooping on this Woody what's his name?"

"It or something like it."

"Shouldn't we get a move on then?" He scanned the walkways above for a way up to the loft. "This Woody Hamburger might come back early from lunch."

"No problem." I tried not to sound smug. "It's Saturday, and I know exactly where he is. Professor Poplov, too. And it's Newburger, not Hamburger."

"You know where they are?" He gave me a doubtful look. "How?"

I grinned. "It's April twelfth."

I could see my little calculator wheels whizzing around in his head.

"April—twelfth," he said slowly. Then he grinned. "My first science fair! That's it, isn't it? This is the year Professor Poplov was there to give out the awards."

"Right. He took his lunch in a paper bag, remember? And was there until midafternoon, because that's when he gave me—you—us our plaque. Come on, there's a ladder to the loft back here." I led the way toward the crates at the far end of the room.

"I wonder whether the box is eavesdropping on us," Jacko whispered as he followed.

I hadn't thought of that. Maybe we'd already said too much. Industrial spies couldn't learn all that much about a technical process just by recording voices, but there had been that wire . . . I made the old kid's game sign of locking my lips, and then looked up at the ceiling.

An iron ladder that was bolted to the side wall about six feet from the back end of the lab led up to a trap door into the attics. From below there wasn't any sign of a lock, so I climbed on up. From close-to you could see that it hadn't been opened in years.

"Painted shut," I mouthed down to Jacko. He only looked puzzled, so I made painting motions, and he nodded.

I still carry around the old Swiss Army pocketknife I got for my tenth birthday, so I could have tried chipping out the paint, but when you've got this shrimpy twelve-year-old self watching, there's a temptation to—well, show him he's not always going to be a pathetic little shrimp. After all, I *did* work out in the exercise room in Oakley Gym three times a week. So I ducked my head, got up on the third rung from the top, tucked my shoulder up against the door, and heaved.

I shouldn't have.

"What's wrong?" Jacko called, forgetting there might be a bug.

"I think I dislocated my shoulder," I wheezed as soon as I could get the words out.

But I hadn't. And when I'd climbed down far enough to get my hand in my pocket, one probe with the old

Swiss Army knife and it was all too clear: the trapdoor was welded shut.

"What are we going to do now?" Jacko whispered when I climbed down and explained.

"There's another hatch out in the front hall, but it has a lock and I don't have a key for it. Even if I did, anybody going past the front door could spot us. And nobody's going to take us for air-conditioning repairmen."

"But we've *got* to get up there."

I scanned the ceiling. There were eight small air-conditioning vents. It would be easy enough to unscrew a vent cover, but even if you were a midget and managed to climb up through the opening, you'd be trapped inside an air-conditioning duct, with no way out into the attic itself.

There was also, for some reason probably to do with whatever the lab was originally used for, an opening supposedly for an extractor fan down at the far end, above the far catwalk. The fan had been missing for as long as I could remember. It was already missing now. I pointed up at the hole.

"How do we get up there?" Jack whispered.

"The empty crates?"

Most of them were big and too heavy to wrestle up onto the catwalk, but a couple of the smaller ones, one on its side, and the other on its end to give me a step up—

Jacko turned a doubtful look up at the square in the ceiling. "It's awfully small," he whispered.

I eyed the opening and then his shoulders, and then the opening again. He was probably right.

"You're right," I whispered back. I wasn't exactly disappointed. This lurking and sneaking stuff was beginning to get to me. "I suggest we leave it to Woody to investigate."

"But how are you going to tell him? You don't know his computer entry code. If you leave a message in the lab files, who knows who might read it?"

I suspected from the anxious look in his eye that what he really meant was that he'd miss out on all the fun. Fun, hah!

"I think it would be best to write him a note. From 'A Friend.' "

"And prop it up on his desk? So he'll think it's one of the lab assistants pulling his leg?"

"A letter, then. On electrical engineering department stationery. There should be letter paper and stamps out in Lab A. We can deposit it in the mailbox across the street, return here, and at 3:00 be transported back where we came from."

"But then we'll never know what happens."

"I suppose you have a better idea?"

"We-e-ell—we do know somebody who might fit that opening."

"Who's that?" I was suspicious, O.K., but I honestly didn't see the bean-ball coming.

Jacko was all wide-eyed innocence.

"What about this little eight-year-old kid who happens to be maybe five hundred yards away, at the science fair over in the university basketball pavilion?"

12

As you will have noticed, I do not seem to have a very efficient self-preservation instinct. To put it another way, however full of brains my head may be, it is not always screwed on right and tight.

Oh, I argued. But I gave in.

We were going to do this, I said, on a Need-to-Know basis. What our "little kid" didn't know, he couldn't tell, right? All he *needed* to know was that we wanted him to climb through a hole in a ceiling and look for something like a black box, O.K.? We were not going to breathe one word more than that, understood? We let him jump to the conclusion that we are his cousins if he wants to; we ask if he wouldn't like to see the inside of a university lab; we tell him I work in one, but to start off, we don't even say which one. Right? Right.

The pavilion floor was packed with rows of booths and display tables and two or three hundred people. The Bay Area Science Fair crowd was thinner than the hordes I vaguely remembered from the Great Day—maybe because it was getting close to lunchtime, maybe because I was two feet taller this time around, and didn't feel so towered-over.

Jacko led the way through the maze of displays of

experiments and working models that crowded the pavilion floor. Not that I didn't remember where my project display had been—right on the free-throw line at the far end. How could I forget? On that spot, at eight years old, at my first science fair, I won a one-thousand-dollar college scholarship and got my picture not only in the local paper but the *San Francisco Chronicle* and the *Los Angeles Times.* But this time around all I felt was dread. The thought of meeting one more me made my stomach feel like it had shrunk to the size of a Ping-Pong ball. A lead Ping-Pong ball.

Not Jacko, though. If I was down, he was up. So up he made me even more nervous. Maybe he managed to hold himself to a walk as we threaded our way across to the middle aisle, but it was a walk with a distinctly enthusiastic bounce to it.

What on earth, I wondered, was the kid going to be like? Do you know, I couldn't remember much about being eight except that I had been nuts about calculus, physics, and "Star Trek" reruns.

Mutt. That's what everybody called me when I was little. My big brother Phil started it, and it stuck. Mutt. Some joke. It was because there's this breed of dog called Jack Russell, in case you don't know. I mean, how undignified can you get?

I looked around for Professor Poplov and after a bit spotted him talking to a little red-haired kid at a display over on the far side of the floor. Woody I didn't see anywhere. I didn't know him back then—back now—but I remembered him saying he'd been to this science fair.

I guess you could say I was dragging my feet—I did

drop pretty far behind Jacko, who was making a fast beeline for "Low-cost Waveform Recorder to Capture Nanosecond-rate Signal Transients for Display and Computer Analysis, John J. Russell, 8th Grade, Dewey Middle School, Shelford, California." I found myself glancing at the exhibits and reading the placards as I passed. I didn't remember ever having seen any of them. Maybe I hadn't looked at them. "Calcium-source Discrimination in Hermit Crabs." "Area Fluctuations in Fractals." "The Function of Inner-surface Proteins in Red-blood-cell-membrane Bonding Sites." "Waveform Recorder . . ."

Waveform Recorder? I backtracked to the table covered with dark blue felt. The title and explanation placards were really classy—done in block letters except for the subtitle in fancy script, but in the kind of block letters a calligrapher does, not a kid. I remembered redoing my title three times because the line of letters kept tilting down the poster board.

"Waveform Recorder," it read. "Maxwell T. Sharp III, Senior, Duxford High School, Duxford, California."

The Shark? *He* had an entry?

I stiffened and cast a quick look around the booth-and-table-crowded floor, half expecting to see his sleek blond head cruising toward me through the crowd like a tall, gray fin through water. But he wasn't anywhere around. Not that I could see, anyway. But I beat it after Jacko at top speed, wondering on the way what Max's display could mean. Or whether it had to mean anything. After all, I never met him before I got to the university. So what if we had worked on the same project and mine walked off with the award? Sheer coincidence. Another one of those "the-idea-is-in-the-air" coincidences the Professor warns about when he wants to light a fire under you. From what I saw, Max's approach to the waveform problem had been different from mine at half a dozen points. So it really does happen. For a minute there I had happily jumped to the conclusion that the Shark might be mixed up in the Poplov Labs mystery. Pure wishful thinking. Too bad.

I was so busy wishing Max was four feet tall with warts and glasses and bad breath that I ran smack into Jacko. We couldn't have been far from our own display, but he was backpedaling like mad.

"What's the matter?"

Jacko dragged me behind a photograph-covered partition. "He's not there. I think he's gone to the john. Remember who's watching the display for him?" He shivered. "This is weirder than I thought it would be. I almost walked up and said, 'I thought you went off to have lunch at the Green Pagoda.' This time-travel stuff is spooky. It was like my brain slipped a gear."

I peered out from behind the partition screen to see what had started him flapping. And no wonder. It was Mom and Dad. I ducked back out of sight like I'd been shot through the gizzard. (I know human beings do not have gizzards. Chickens have gizzards. But 'shot through the stomach' sounds revolting. I prefer the light touch.)

Let me tell you, I could have used a light touch right then. A weak smile. A lame joke, even. Oh, off and on so far I'd been scared, frantic, uneasy, desperate, you name it, but I hadn't felt like, um—leaking saline fluid into the old eyes out of the lachrymal glands. An awful, lower-than-the-pits feeling rolled over me. *If I get stuck here and now, I've lost Mom and Dad and Phil. They'll belong to Mutt-me, not ME-me.*

Funny thing. Jacko didn't seem fazed at all. I guess it was because they didn't look all that much different to him. But to me they looked so *young*. It was creepy. When you're around people all the time, it's like they never get any older. But there was Dad with all his hair, and Mom without the gray in hers. I'd got used to seeing Dad next thing to bald, he was so thin on top.

I had to get home. No two ways about it.

"Are they still there?"

Jacko stuck his head out. "Yes. But guess what? I see Mo and Polly, too."

"Where?" I looked where he was pointing—back the way we had come—and there was the little red-haired kid I'd seen talking to Professor Poplov. Maureen Dilley. Mo. Her family moved to San Diego when I was ten. I'd forgotten what a funny-looking little kid she'd been—green eyes, copper-red hair, braces, wall-to-wall freckles, skinny, bouncing all over the place. She was wearing a Sylvester the Cat T-shirt, and Band-Aids on both elbows.

But Polly was—Polly. Back when I was eight I never paid any attention to what she looked like, but this was weird. The only way she looked much different from the Polly I knew was that she was smaller. Ten-year-old size.

We couldn't hear what they were arguing about, but

I guess Polly was acting sniffy and superior. Mo looked ready to shoot sparks. Then, whatever happened happened so fast that I couldn't tell who did what to whom. According to Jacko, Polly pinched Mo and Mo yelled bloody murder, but when the people standing nearest turned around, there was Polly, tears sliding down her cheeks, clutching *her* arm. Mo stalked off in one direction, and Polly flounced off in the other.

Jacko pulled at my jacket sleeve. "Hey, all clear. Come on." He was bouncing up and down on the balls of his feet like it was all some game and he was itching to get off the sidelines.

"You go," I said. "Forget about the cousin bit; tell him whatever you have to get him to come. The whole thing, for all I care. The faster we find the proof somebody's after Woody's project and report it and get out of here, the better."

I stood there and watched him waltz up to this little dark-haired kid in blue jeans and a Dr. Who T-shirt: a little kid I last saw in the mirror when I was brushing my teeth eight years ago. Then Jacko was talking and waving his hands around, and the little kid was goggling at me, round-eyed as a fish. As if I was the original Thing from Outer Space. I decided I'd better find out what Jacko *was* saying.

". . . and he has an I.D. to prove it, too, only the date on his is *eight* years from now." Finishing triumphantly, Jacko turned to me. "Show him."

"For Pete's sake!" I yelped. "Do you want everyone

and his Uncle Pugwash to hear you?" I looked over my shoulder nervously.

I saw only three people near enough to have heard anything—a youngish couple and a sleek, brainy-looking blond woman wearing five or six gold rings and an expensive-looking suit. The guy looked oddly familiar, but then he was middle-sized, with dark hair, a mustache, brown cords, a sleeveless down jacket, like maybe a half a thousand other guys on campus. The three of them were too deep in talk to have heard anything. I caught the word "Galaxitronics" once, but couldn't make out anything else, so figured it was safe to bet they couldn't have heard Jacko unless they were lip-readers.

"You can't go around broadcasting things like that," I hissed. "They'll throw us in the booby bin. And *then* where will Poplov Labs be?"

But I did pull out my wallet to show Mutt my university I.D. card.

At that he stopped goggling and narrowed his eyes.

"It could be forged," he said slowly. "But nobody but me ever says 'everyone and his Uncle Pugwash.' I made that up. Just yesterday. So—"

You could see him trying to swallow the idea. Personally, I felt for the poor kid. It must have been like trying to swallow a grapefruit. Whole.

"If I go with you," he said at last—like we'd asked him out for pizza and a Coke, "I have to be back before two-thirty. For the awards. I think the judges like my project. And Mom and Dad are coming back then."

Jacko was about to blurt out exactly how much the

judges liked the project, but I shut him up with a look. Why shouldn't the kid enjoy the suspense and surprise? We had. At least, *I* had.

I took a quick look at my watch and announced, "The time is—five minutes to one. The lab building in question is located only a short distance from here. You should be back by two. Two-fifteen at the very latest."

The little kid—I guess I'll have to call him Mutt too—turned to whisper to Jacko. "Does he always talk that way? Like he went to the laundry and got starched?"

Jacko blinked, and then blushed when he saw I had heard. You would think that since he had been working all year on sounding more grown-up and intellectual himself, he could have explained. But no, he just nodded and said, "You should have heard him at first."

I cleared my throat and pointed at my watch.

Mutt looked at the two of us doubtfully. What he was thinking was as clear as if it was lettered on a cartoon balloon drawn above his head. He was hearing Mom's old familiar warning, *Never go off anywhere with strangers.*

"For goodness' sake . . ." I began.

"For gosh sakes, *go*!" snapped a new voice.

I jumped. Sure enough, it was Maureen. Mo the Pest.

"I thought you went off to lunch with my folks," Mutt said. "How long have you been listening?"

She ignored the question. "I still haven't seen everything, so I stayed. Besides, I had a hamburger before I came."

She stood there, this little eight year old with her fists

on her hips, and looked me over. "All that stuff about being from the future is silly," she said to Mutt. "I bet you they're your cousins. The ones your mom says might move out here from back East. That one looks sort of like Phil, but he talks funny. He isn't like you."

"Then how come you say 'go'?" put in Jacko.

"Because." Mo dropped her voice. "Because people *do* steal ideas and inventions and designs and things. Daddy says that at the company where he works they have to worry all the time about it. Besides, Professor Poplov is a friend of Daddy's. If somebody's after his invention ideas, then we've got to help."

" 'We'?" I scowled.

She shrugged and turned to Mutt. "O.K. So I'll stay and guard your recorder-thing until your mom and dad get back."

Mutt drew himself up and took a deep breath. "I'll come," he said to Jacko. "And *I* believe it about the time travel. Will I get to see your Tardis?"

I cringed. "*Keep your voice down!*"

"Well, will I?" he whispered.

"No," Jacko whispered back. "There's a machine, but we don't exactly travel *in* it. You see—"

"Will you shut up?" I hissed.

He gave me his baffled look, and all I could do was raise my eyes to the ceiling, and turn to lead the way out. Had I really been such a science-fiction nut? Star Wars lunch box? Dr. Who and his Tardis time machine? I suppose we were lucky—it meant Mutt really wanted to believe us. But it was embarrassing.

Behind me as we went out the front entrance, Jacko was going on about a book we had read by some university professor in England who had a lot to say about the Tardis. What *I* remembered about the book was that it was one of the ones that said travel into the past was impossible. Didn't I wish! Just wait, I thought. Just wait until Jacko catches on that solving the Poplov Labs mystery here and now is bound to change more things in the future than we want changed. Maybe enough to bend our future totally out of shape.

The Poplov Laboratories were an easy five-minute walk from the basketball pavilion—easy for me, at least, but then my legs were longer. Jacko hurried behind, and Mutt scurried to keep up, bringing up the rear as I angled across Malcolm Street and turned onto Bowdoin. I pretended I didn't know them—the one time I looked back was enough. A couple of students going the other way had turned to stare at Meeny, Miney, and Mo playing follow the leader. I found myself getting thoroughly paranoid. Who knows? Maybe—maybe they'd come from the lab building. Maybe they were in on the plot. Assuming I was right and there was one at this point in time. They might not be students at all. Maybe they'd been on watch at the labs, and seen Jacko and me sneak out the door by the loading dock . . .

I walked faster still. The sooner we were safe out of sight, the happier I'd be. Mom and Dad would be coming back after lunch, and who knows which of the four possible routes onto campus they would take from town? What if they came driving along Bowdoin Street and saw three John James Russells—pint, quart, and gallon size—steaming along the sidewalk?

Jacko caught up with me two blocks down Bowdoin Street. His cheerful look was gone.

"J. J.? Mutt says someone's following us!"

13

"Who? Where?"

I didn't see anybody coming our way except Mutt himself, halfway down the block. "Did you see who?"

"No. But Mutt says he's been following ever since we left the fair."

"I can't see anyone. But we'd better not take a chance."

I was surprised at how calm I sounded. I sure didn't feel calm. I turned to walk on. "Come on. Walk slowly until Mutt catches up. Then we can try to lose whoever it is. Do you know the shortcut through the service areas up behind the earth sciences building? Good. Once we pass the bend in the street, we make a dash for the main entrance of earth sciences. If it turns out to be locked, we make an end run around the near corner."

"Right." Jacko dropped back four or five paces.

By the time we reached the bend in the street, Mutt had caught up. As he came past the end of the hedge that ran back between the earth sciences and chemistry building, Jacko and I each grabbed an arm and ran, half lifting him between us.

"Keep quiet!" I warned.

"And for Pete's sake, lift your feet up," Jacko panted.

You could hear the toes of little Mutt's shoes scuffing along, *tunket-ti-tunkit*.

I was worried that the door would be locked and we'd have to run all the way around, but we were in luck. Some professor or grad student must have come in to do some Saturday work. Anyhow, the lock was on the catch. Jacko headed straight down the hall for the back door and the shortcut with the kid right behind him, but after I locked the door I moved to the window beside it to peer out through the open Venetian blind. A minute later Jacko and Mutt came zipping back to find out where I'd got to.

"If we *are* being followed, I want to see by whom," I explained, keeping my eye on the sidewalk.

Jacko headed for the window on the other side of the door.

"Don't touch the blind," Mutt warned. "He'll see."

Maybe, I thought as out of the corner of my eye I saw Jacko grin, the kid was O.K. At least, he wasn't totally in space orbit. On TV the way the dumb detectives and crooks are always opening curtains or bending the blinds to look out always makes me grit my teeth. As if a waggling curtain wasn't a dead giveaway! Funny . . . of *course* if I'd always noticed that, so would Mutt. And Jacko. But it was impossible not to think of them as—as *other* people. Self-preservation, maybe. Otherwise, it is highly possible I would have ended up in a handy corner going *blurble-blurble-blurble*.

"That's him. That's him!" Mutt crowed softly.

"Him" was a dark-haired man, maybe in his late

twenties—the mustache-and-sleeveless-down-jacket guy from the science fair. He slowed down when he saw we weren't up ahead, then stopped and looked all around. Funny—I couldn't be sure because he was standing in the shade of the tree out front, but he really did look familiar. Not just ordinary. The wiry, athletic type. Short dark hair. Hiking boots. Not your TV-series industrial spy. And I *had* seen him somewhere before—besides the science fair. I knew it but couldn't put my finger on the where or when. In the end, he took off across the street and disappeared down the alley beyond the chemistry building.

"All clear," Jacko announced.

"I don't like it," I said. "Have you ever seen him before?"

"Not me."

Mutt hadn't either, but I still didn't like it.

As it turned out, I had other problems.

Oh, we made it out the back door of earth sciences, O.K. And up the back service alley, around the back of the Plant Research Institute, and across the street and the Poplov Labs parking area to the door beside the loading dock. No problem.

But my key didn't fit the lock.

I tried it again. I tried it upside down. I even tried the front-door key. Nothing.

Mutt began to look suspicious. Jacko turned pale.

I swallowed, and then turned to ask Jacko in a casual croak, "You—you wouldn't happen to have noticed when we were on our way out whether the locks on the outside of the lab doors were electronic ones, would you?"

"No." He turned even paler. "We were in such a hurry . . ."

"S'all right," I said hastily. "Don't panic. No need to panic. We—We'll go in the front door instead. No problem."

(Pause for scuttling around to the front of the building.)

(Further pause for trying key every way but backward.)

(Sickening pause while truth sinks in.)

The old locks—the ones in place when Professor Poplov took over the labs—hadn't been changed yet. I had the new keys and these were the old locks. I sat down on the low wall that bordered the sidewalk. I think I moaned.

"What do we do now?" Jacko asked shakily.

Mutt was baffled. "What is it?" he demanded. "What's wrong?"

"It's too complicated. You don't really want to know."

"Maybe he doesn't, but *I* do," said another, unexpected voice.

With that, the guy who'd been tailing us stepped out from behind the big redwood tree.

The voice, at least, I knew.

"*Woody!*"

It was Woody Newburger, all right. The pale blue eyes and astonished eyebrows, at least, were the same.

Even so, I had a hard time matching this Woody up with the skinny, unmustached, unshaven, baggy-trousered one I knew, the Woody with his shoes run over at the heels and the raggle-taggle haircut. *This* was Woody Newburger?

"You *are* Woody? Woody Newburger?"

His eyebrows flew even higher. "I am. Do I know you?"

"Well, uh, yes—but not yet."

I think I grinned when I said it. Lame joke. But Woody's eyes narrowed and positively glittered as he looked the three of us up and down and over.

"And who would you three be?"

"I'm Mutt Russell," Mutt said before either of us could dig him with a warning elbow. "And that's Jacko, and he's J. J. . . ."

"I see. Brothers, I take it."

"Ye-es."

"Amazing. Brothers. Same hairline. Same mole. Same scar. Very unusual, wouldn't you say? Even my girl noticed. When you trooped out of the pavilion all in a row, she said, 'Look—Micro, Mini, and Maxi.' "

That cracked Mutt up, but he smothered the giggles when I glared at him.

Woody crossed his arms. "All right. We're introduced. Now I want to know why you've been trying to break into the Poplov Labs."

"It's not really breaking in when you have a key," Mutt ventured. "Is it?"

"That depends. Let's see this key." He held out his hand.

What could I do? I handed my key ring over.

Talk about eyes glittering—Woody took one look at the front-door key and gave a shiver like he was glittering all over with excitement.

"*Chubb. 27PL12. Do not duplicate,*" he read. Then he looked up and said in this shaky voice, "Where in—where on earth did you get this? We only sent the order off yesterday for these special new Chubb locks. And that's the marking I ordered. For Building twenty-seven. Poplov Labs. Door number one. Key number two. You can't possibly *have* this key."

You could have cut the silence into slices, it was so thick.

Mutt broke it first. "Look, it's almost one-thirty," he said uneasily. "I think maybe you'd better tell him."

Jacko agreed nervously. "After all, it is his research project that gets—that could get stolen."

"Stolen? *My* project? My dissertation?" Woody's voice rose a couple of notes higher with each word.

What choice did I have? We had to get into the lab, and Woody had the keys. So I explained about the cherry picker and the movable roof panel. I tried to make it sound as if when we saw it "last night," it had been his here-and-now last night, but he listened with a fierce, squinty-eyed, faraway look that made me nervous. A sort of Aha!-Is-that-a-cockroach-I-see-in-the-corner? look. Had Woody maybe been a little bit loony all along? Even before he lost his girl and hit the bottle? I was pretty sure of it when he reached out and grabbed at Mutt's hand.

"You two, too. Show me your right hands. Palm up," he ordered.

I didn't catch on to what bee he had in his bonnet until I saw our three palms side by side. They all three had the same life line running down around the base of the thumb. The same heart line. Star lines. Head line. Palms, in case you don't know, are like fingerprints: no two exactly alike. It gave me the creeps all over again.

The funny thing was, Woody didn't say Word One. I couldn't figure him. He just dropped Mutt's hand and the whole thing. He fished his keys out of his pocket. Looked to see that the coast was clear. Unlocked the front door and herded us in. Got a ladder out of the utility cupboard in the back hall. Climbed up to unlock the ceiling trap door (I had never noticed there was one) in the storeroom nearest the loading dock. And once he had told Mutt and Jacko where to find the light switch up above, they were up the ladder into the attic in a flash.

"Will they really know what to look for?"

I nodded. "Jacko does anyway." Better not to say he was an electrical engineering student. Whatever Woody suspected, he couldn't *know*. But he would know there wasn't any twelve year old in the department. Yet.

That's me every time: shutting the stable door after the horses are out. Because as soon as we saw a light switch on above and heard Mutt and Jacko move away from the trap door, Woody sat down on a handy crate. Suddenly. As if his knees had gone mushy.

His whisper was hoarse.

"It's Pandora's Box, isn't it? Pandora's Box brought you here."

14

Woody paced nervously up and down between the storeroom shelves, looking more scared than excited. I began to worry what there was I ought to be worrying about that I hadn't caught onto yet.

Woody shook his head. "I was sure it was crazy. I never thought it would work. Never!"

"The Box, you mean?"

He nodded wildly.

"But what ever made you think the Box had anything to do with *us*? Me, I mean." I peered down at my tie and blazer and polished loafers. It wasn't as if I was walking around in a Buck Rogers tunic and tights.

Woody threw me this funny grin. "Oh, no fear. You could probably pass inspection all the way back to 1950."

So what was funny in that?

But already he was looking anxious again. "No, it's not that either of you look 'out of the future.' Who knows? I guess after the Professor's 'what if's,' my subconscious must have thought about the possibilities a lot more than I did. The awful truth just flashed on me while I was talking to Dr. Mona Crawford, Galaxitronics' research director, when Doris—my girl—giggled and pointed at the three of you trooping out through the fair exhibits. Same walk, same set of the shoulders, same chin sticking out. Same mole—even pretty much the same haircut. It was so eerie I thought maybe I'd cracked at last. Then after you headed off in this direction, I decided maybe, just maybe, I hadn't fallen off my rocker after all. When I checked your palms, I knew for sure."

"O.K.," I said. "I could buy—er, I might be able to accept that. But I still don't see how you can know about the Box. Professor Poplov can't have started work on it—*won't* start work on it for another two years or so."

Woody zipped up his jacket zipper and then nervously pulled it down and zipped it up again. And again. Down-up. Down-up. I don't think he knew he was doing it.

"The Box was just a wild idea the Professor and I tossed around two or three years ago in a couple of our brainstorming sessions," he explained. "But the computer and high-energy technology weren't up to it. Still aren't. Won't be for another twenty years or more."

He stopped his pacing, turned and stared at me intently. "Or will they? You look much too young to be a grad student, but you must be if you work here in whatever time you come from. How old *are* you? Seventeen? Eighteen?"

"Well, almost seventeen."

"Sixteen? Great balls of fire! Let's see—if the little one of you—Mutt?—is eight or nine . . . but that's impossible. How can the Box be operational in less than ten years? That would mean energy capacities will grow far faster than—"

"They do," I agreed. "About three years from now there will be a twenty-trillion-watt K-laser. And in eight years Professor Poplov will be able to, ah, 'borrow' the power to pump up Pandora's Box from Galaxitronics' oversupply. Once their X-ray Galaxitron is completely on-line, they say it will generate something like 100 trillion watts. *And* the Professor has been working on a high-energy version of his old PowerJack. It ought to triple the energy input into our klasers. It . . ."

"Enough! Don't tell me." Woody had gone pale around the gills.

"Why not?"

He shook his head decidedly. "It's not safe. Once you know what's coming, you can work to make it happen faster. Too fast. Before the world can handle it. No, thanks. I'd rather take the future as it comes."

Now, this attitude, I clearly saw (if you could say I was capable of seeing anything clearly), was going to present a problem. Including, what about his girlfriend, Doris the Deserter? He needed to know what a walking disaster area she was, but should we tell him? If the research pirates were caught, before long old Woody would be Dr. Woodrow Newburger and—who knows?—maybe get to be rich and famous. Or at least well-off and well-known. And Doris the Deserter would definitely not desert. She would marry him, and the poor guy might never find out she had a pocket calculator for a heart.

"I see your point," I said, trying to sound like I saw it but knew an Awful Truth that made hash out of it.

He flapped his hands like he was Pandora in the old story, batting away the cloud of nasties that came swarming up out of the Horrible Box.

"No buts. I—" He stopped short and skewered me

with an anxious stare. "You haven't told anybody else any of this. *Tell* me you haven't told anybody else."

"Only Jacko. And he told Mutt. But not all of it. Only enough to get him over here."

"That's good. Yes, good." Woody went back to his pacing. "But can Mutt be counted on to keep his mouth shut? If he's only eight, he won't understand how important it is. I mean, how can he?"

"He's very intelligent," I said huffily.

But Woody was already back to shaking his head over Professor Poplov.

"How *could* he go ahead with Pandora's Box? Sheer curiosity, I suppose. Sometimes it gets him like a disease. But he knows perfectly well the Box is too dangerous. Once word got out, he said, everybody and his dog would be foaming at the mouth to go back in time. All the wrong people. Even all the *right* people would be wrong people. Coming back and making our choices for us." He glowered at me as if I were the fulfillment of a nasty prophecy. Which I suppose I was.

"Heh, heh." I laughed weakly. "Um. Maybe without you around to niggle at his conscience he argued himself around to 'All Knowledge of Itself Is Good'?"

Me and my big mouth. As soon as the words came out I thought, Oh, glurk, now I've put my foot in it. What happens when he asks *why* he wasn't around? Maybe I could just say that he would up and quit graduate school after his research project evaporated. I decided I didn't have the heart to tell him about Doris the Deserter. When in doubt go for half the truth.

Woody nodded. "Could be. I admit I've worried about what he might get up to after I finish my degree. But I'll be close by, so I'll be able to keep an eye on him. I've had two job offers already, from Galaxitronics and Macro Research, and they're both local. So what—"

I was sure he was going to say, "So what happens? Why *don't* I stick around and steer the Professor away from the Box?" I was saved by Jacko's loud "*Gotcha!*" from overhead.

Mutt's dust-smudged face appeared over the edge of the trap door. He wore a wide grin. "We found it!"

"A bug?" Woody and I asked together.

Jacko appeared on the other side of the opening.

"Maybe. There's a relay transmitter tucked in under the eaves. It's in a black case. The one we saw. And there's a wire that goes from it along a floorboard crack all the way over to a little hole that's got to be above Lab B."

"I pulled at it," Mutt put in. "But it's fastened somewhere."

"Right." Woody was grim. "You two stay up there. Nobody's likely to come in here, but you'd better close that hatch. Then get back to where the wire disappears. Give us a minute, and then start tapping. We'll try to locate the spot from below."

It didn't take long. The wire had been fed down into the partition wall between Labs A and B. And guess which section of wall? Right. Smack behind Woody's computer workstation. And what it was attached to hadn't been put there from the attic.

Down under the desk, where the terminal's cable was coupled into the wall socket that joined it to the university computer's linkup system, faint lines along the plasterboard showed that a foot-square section had been cut out, replaced, glued, smoothed at the seams, and repainted. Woody banged a hole in its middle with a hammer and ripped it out. Inside, we found what was at the end of the wire from the attic: a black plastic whatsis the size of a box of kitchen matches clamped around the linkup feeder cable right where it came out of the back of the wall socket.

Woody backed out from under the desk and first Jacko crawled under for a look, then Mutt.

"The nerve!" Jacko fumed. "They've tapped right into the terminal."

Mutt stuck his head in the hole. "What is it? Some kind of modem?"

"No." Woody frowned. "The system security can detect unauthorized hook-ins. But it may come to the same thing. My guess is it's a sensor of some kind. A hypersensitive one that can read electronic impulses right through the cable insulation. Whoever is on the receiver end of that transmitter must have every bit of data I've recorded. Every computation I've made."

A couple of things that had baffled me began to make sense—one in particular.

"*That*'s it!" I said. "It must be about four years from now—after someone stole a jump on his hyperlaser—that Professor Poplov started on his deep security kick and put the electronic locks on the inner doors. Once they got wind of that, they wouldn't risk his checking the lab and finding their bug. They figured nobody would find this thing. But they pulled out the bug. While Jacko and I were watching."

"I bet the little black box they left behind where that transmitter is now was some new supertransmitter," Jacko suggested. "I bet that's how you got stung too."

I blinked. "Max the Shark and my Translat program, you mean? I don't think so. Not with his connection to the lab. That would be flat out asking for trouble. No, it was just rotten luck. Max and I have been on the same wavelength before. Today, in fact, at the science fair. There's another waveform recorder project—not really anything like mine—and it's his. I never connected Max with it because I never met him until we were in plasma physics class together."

"The science fair!" Mutt backed out from under the computer terminal desk and jumped up so suddenly that he cracked his head against it. "Ow! What time is it? Gosh, two-*thirty*? I've got to get back."

I grabbed at him. "Not so fast—you can't go over there looking like somebody's used you for a dust mop." I brushed him down and Jacko used spit and a couple of tissues to wipe the attic dust off the kid's face.

Once the front door closed after Mutt, we stood and watched him tear across the street and out of sight.

Woody drew a deep breath.

"Now, what about this Max Sharp?"

"Forget him." I followed him back down the hall to the labs. "The real question is, Who placed the sensor in the first place?"

Woody made a face. I think he already didn't like the answer.

"The terminal was there before Professor Poplov took over the building," he said thoughtfully. "And the two lab assistants only have keys to the outer door and Lab A. They don't work in B or C unless the Professor or I are there. So they couldn't have fiddled with the cable. And nobody else has access . . ."

"So?"

"So," he said slowly, "it had to be somebody who worked here when the university still ran these labs. 'The Brain Bin,' we called it back then. There were four professors besides Poplov—Peek, Plant, Short, and Gaborik—and six research assistants besides me. Professor Short wanted from the first to form a private research and development company, and once he found a backer, they started setting up Galaxitronics."

"Did everybody but you and Professor Poplov go in on it?" Jacko asked.

"Everybody else but Professor Peek and a grad student named Woffington. Woof Woffington."

Woof? But I was not to be distracted. "That leaves eight. Eight suspects."

"Eight? More like eighteen. Twenty-eight. They had workmen in and out all through the move up to the new Galaxitronics complex. And it stood empty for three months before the university agreed to lease the building to Professor Poplov. The business office people were in and out. The university's maintenance men too. Probably Professor Poplov's insurance agent. Take your pick." Woody sat down at the computer terminal.

With two or three dozen possible suspects, one thing was sure. The mystery wasn't going to be tidied up by three o'clock. Or even by midnight.

"But we have only until twelve tonight," I protested.

"Don't worry. It shouldn't be hard to flush them out." Woody began clicking away at his keyboard. "I'm leaving a memo in the Professor's 'Today' file, and their sensor ought to pick it up as it goes out."

We leaned over his shoulders to watch as the message peeped its way across the screen:

> EUREKA! PROJECT DATA & COMPUTATION COMPLETE. WILL ENTER FINAL CHAPTER ON TERMINAL AT HOME TONIGHT & DO REMOTE PRINTOUT OF COMPLETE DISSERTATION ON E.E. OFFICE PRINTER. SHOULD FINISH & PICK UP BEFORE MIDNIGHT, GET IT TO YOU TOMORROW A.M. ! !

"There. If they think the write-up of the whole project will be going out over the linkup system from my terminal in the dorm to the printer in the department office, my guess is they'll try to break into the office and use one of their sensors to tap the printer cable. The Professor won't have any problem getting the police to set up a trap. Not with his clout."

I was never so relieved in my life. "Great. We can leave all that to you, then." I looked at my watch, and grinned at Jacko. "Twenty to three. In twenty-five minutes the Box will be taking us home." *Home.* Home, with my computer program finished before Max's, the

Professor's klaser design saved, and Woody rescued from the bottle, if not from Doris.

"Twenty to three!" Woody leaped up from his desk chair. "I've got to get over to the pavilion before Professor Poplov finishes speechifying to the award winners, or he'll be off and away and I'll never be able to round him up."

"You're going to tell him?" Jacko asked uneasily. He had good reason to be uneasy. Once Professor Poplov learned that I had broken into the Box's cupboard, when the time came, he'd be about as likely to take Jacko on as a research assistant as King Kong.

"If I leave him out of tonight's fun, he'll never forgive me. Besides," Woody said as he unlocked Lab C and shoved us in, "I'll be back in a trisket."

"A 'trice,' " I corrected automatically.

Woody looked pained. "Whatever. Anyhow, don't go off at three if I'm not back." He shut the door behind him.

"Oh, sure." I kicked at a handy packing crate. "Stick around here and see if we can't gum my life up a little bit more."

"You mean, go off even if Mutt doesn't get back to say good-bye?"

" 'Good-bye' is hardly the word, pea brain. Mutt is going to grow up to *be* us two."

I heard Jacko mutter something to himself. But what it sounded like didn't make any sense.

It *sounded* like "You wanna bet?"

15

I shouldn't have been surprised that Jacko was all for hanging around to see the fireworks. How could I blame him? A midnight break-in, a police ambush. Woody's research rescued, and Professor Poplov's klaser to be saved into the bargain? I was tempted myself.

But not much.

"*I*'m going, so I hardly see that you have a choice," I said stiffly. "Not if you want to get back where you started from."

"Why can't I stay?" he wheedled. "And you go on ahead, I mean. The Box's already programmed for both recalls, and it won't make more than a couple of minutes' difference at your end. It's not like you'd have to wait around for me for nine hours. You said as soon as it finishes one recall, it resets and starts the next one, so I'd be right behind you."

"Not a chance. I'm not leaving you here to get us into who knows what new mess. You're coming. *And*," I announced in triumph, "once we get there, I send you back at five-thirty your time. In plenty of time to get ready for Polly's birthday party. You won't have to miss it this time around. Everything will be back on track!" It was so simple, so beautiful, and seemed so perfect that I marveled I hadn't thought of it before.

He gave me this weird look. At least it struck me as weird at the time. It was—well, pitying. Like the look you might give a poor dumb groundhog who got creamed when he tried to cross an interstate highway. I couldn't figure it.

Not that it mattered. If I said he had to come, he had to come.

The next twenty minutes were pretty grim. I pulled the old lab stool up near where the Box's time window would appear, and settled down to wait. Considering that I was doing the sensible thing, you would think that sooner or later Jacko would have to give up and admit as much. But, no. All he did was dawdle around the big lab, peering up at the steel catwalks and poking his nose into control panels, packing cases, and storage lockers. Ignoring me. Which meant I had plenty of time to (a) worry whether, after all that had happened, maybe the time window wouldn't turn up at all, and (b) work around to the point of wondering exactly what he'd meant by that "You wanna bet?" crack. I began to be uneasy. How could Mutt *not* want to grow up to be Jacko and me?

I never got any further than wondering. The Box's patch of shadow began to grow in Lab C's late afternoon gloom.

Let me tell you, I was so relieved I was half afraid to get down from the stool for fear my knees would go *floop*. O.K., I did wonder for a second or two why the shadow should be dark—why it should be nighttime instead of just after 5:30 in the time that was waiting for us on the other side of the window, but the recall had worked. That was what mattered. The timer on my watch was already set at ten minutes, but my fingers were so wobbly it took four or five tries before I could set it going.

Jacko saw it too. The window, that is.

"O.K., O.K., I'm coming. Keep your socks on," he grumbled.

An arthritic snail would have got there faster. And when he did, he still stalled.

"How much time do we have? Woody and Mutt might still come."

"Nine minutes. No, eight and a bit. But I'm not taking any chances. Come on." Not that I didn't trust him, but I caught at his wrist and pulled him toward the time window.

Jacko held back. "Cut it out, J. J. Listen! Somebody's coming."

I pulled harder, and got one foot part way in the window. "Sure they are."

But then I heard it too.

A far-off grumble of voices, out in the hall or Lab A.

Whoever it was must have barged on in to Lab B, for in the next breath we heard a loud, indignant protest.

"And who are you, Woodrow Newburger, to make an order to Nicholas Poplov he cannot enter his own laboratory? I have never heard such a nonsense!" Professor Poplov's bad-tempered bellow boomed right through the four-inch-thick lab door.

Now, if it had been up to me, I would have sailed through the Box's window in a single bound (as they say). But I couldn't. Not only had half my foot gone to sleep, but Jacko was, to put it mildly, not cooperating. He was pulling like crazy in one direction, trying to get loose, but he kept panting out, "Look! Mutt!" and flapping his free arm the other way, toward the lab windows.

I didn't let loose, but I looked. Sure enough, there was the kid, high up in one of the trees alongside the parking lot, waving his arms at us like a windmill in a hurricane.

"He means 'Stop,' " Jacko panted. He tugged harder. "Something's gone wrong."

"It's perfectly obvious something is about to go wrong, you idiot. He means 'Hurry up.' " I gnashed my teeth in frustration (which, I can tell you, is not just something villains do in comic books—GNASH! GNASH!). And numb toes or no, I lunged further into the shadow, with Jacko still dragging like an anchor.

The door from Lab B swung open.

"What on the good green earth . . . ?"

For maybe the first and the last time in his entire life, Professor Poplov was struck speechless. I was, you might say, too busy at the time to notice, but to hear Woody tell it afterward, at the sight of Jacko and me—and the weird black-as-night shadow hanging there in midair—the Professor went as white as his beard. His mouth shaped words that didn't come out. And then (so says Woody, who was scared spitless) his eyes began to glow. Sort of like—well, imagine a cross between Jolly Old Saint Nick and Dr. Frankenstein. To Woody's relief, the glow faded after a moment or two, and

Professor Poplov shook himself like a dog who's just come out of the water.

"Stop!" he croaked. "You, young man! Move away. Quickly!"

I didn't move away. So he bellowed.

"Come away! Numbskull! Do you not see? *There is no There there!"*

But I couldn't. I had let go of Jacko, and I was falling.

16

Believe me, nothing but nothing is scarier than *nothing*. Unless it's feeling yourself toppling over into it. All that while I thought the foot I had stuck through the Box's window had fallen asleep—I could feel my heel, but it was like the rest of my size eleven wasn't there. Then when I lunged to go through the window, it was the same all the way down my right side. Not numb. With numb you get prickles. This was *not there*. I heard Professor Poplov's warning shout, but I was already teetering on the lone foot that was still in the lab, and then my head started fuzzing up. Fuzzing up? Actually, it was more like a slow-motion version of what happens when you turn your TV off: everything narrowing down to a thin line that sucks itself up into a bright dot. Somewhere in there I let go of Jacko's wrist and this story nearly got itself a considerably different ending.

What happened was, Jacko yelled, "Look out!" and they all lunged at once. He got my wrist, Professor Poplov caught at my coattail, and Woody sailed through the air in what Mutt, watching from his tree, said was a spectacular lateral tackle. When I came to, we were piled up on the floor, and it felt like I had half the Chicago Bears backfield draped across me. The Professor, to put it delicately, is no shrimp.

Then they were all up and jabbering in alarm, anger, and explanation. Somebody hauled up a desk chair and they all three hoisted me up and propped me in it, but it was a while before I could get myself together. And that's no figure of speech. I felt like my whole right side had been disconnected. Not in the electrical sense. Well, maybe it was a little like having a power brownout. But the zapped half of me felt *separate*, too. Like it was sitting maybe a yard away instead of glued to the left half, where it belonged. A sensation like that, let me tell you, is enough to blow anybody's fuse.

While Jacko and Professor Poplov were hovering over me, waiting for me to say something more than *aww-wrk* and wondering whether they ought to send for an ambulance, Woody went out to fetch Mutt in before the sight of him up his tree attracted any unwelcome attention. So when my eyes uncrossed and decided to cooperate with each other, and I managed to croak out, "Wha' was that?" the kid was hanging onto my arm, peering at me anxiously. Since most of the time until then he'd eyed me like I had pointed ears, or—no, more like I had a bad case of pinkeye and he was afraid of catching it, I figured I must look as sick as I felt.

"What was it? The Great Nothing," Professor Poplov rumbled. He mopped his brow with a bandanna handkerchief and tried to hide his relief in gruffness. "The Nowhere. How am I to know?"

"But—but J. J. was going *some*where," Jacko protested. "If it was nowhere, we couldn't have pulled back out the half of him that fell in."

"Perhaps—perhaps." Professor Poplov tugged thoughtfully at his beard, but then turned to glower at me.

"Young idiot! Why did you think to do so rash a thing? If as your young friend here says, you have come here by some time device, then surely you have left your wits behind you. It is clear that you have done something in this here-and-now which has changed what is to come. Because of this change, your device has—how shall I say?—been interrupted in its work. Perhaps, even, this device will now not come to exist."

I couldn't wrap my head around that one. It—my head—felt like it was stuffed full of absorbent cotton. All I could do was sit there opening and shutting my mouth like some goggle-eyed goldfish. I couldn't even manage a squeak to stop Jacko spilling the crucial bean.

He had turned pale.

"But Pandora's Box *does* exist. It's got to!"

Woody cringed. With Professor Poplov you edge up sideways on a ticklish subject and nudge him in at the shallow end. You do not make a run at him and butt him off the side.

"*Pandora's Box?*" The Professor's beard bristled out fiercely and his face and bald pate went from Santa-Claus pink to an alarming plum color.

As soon as I could manage a wheeze, it all had to come out. All the Box stuff at least, from that first accidental glimpse I got of the Jacko-Me. When I came to describing the Box itself, the Professor ordered Woody, Jacko, and Mutt—whose ears had been flapping like mad—out into Lab B.

"What you do not know," he pronounced as he held open the door for them, "will not do you damage."

When Professor Poplov had heard what little I had to tell about the Box's design and operation, he huffed and puffed and snuffled and snorted.

"I do not believe it. I cannot believe it. But what you describe—I have imagined just such a hyperlaser as these K-lasers you speak of. Yet how can *I* build such a thing as Pandora's Box? I, who see so clearly the dreadful dangers!" He harrumphed and pulled thoughtfully at his beard. "I, of course, knowing the dangers and being the most cautious of men, could use such a device. But let the world know such a thing exists, and the world will steal it. Either by theft or by law. And if well-meaning blunderers or the curious who do not understand what great effects can come from small causes—if such persons of goodwill may turn the world toward ill, then think what evils may come if others visit the past to turn events so that they may win riches or power. Only think! No, I can never, must never develop such a device!"

He stood with his hands in his pockets and his beard jutting out, daring me to say boo.

But I couldn't not say it. "Yes, sir. I mean no, sir. You are right about the Box. I can see that now. But you *will* build it. Jacko and I are the proof. I'm here. Jacko's here."

"Hum. So you are. So you are." He stumped up and down, deep in thought, for a couple of minutes before he went to the door to order the others back in.

"All is clear what must be done," he announced, stroking his beard the way he does when he lectures in class. I held my breath.

"It has been clear to me since first Pandora's Box was spoken of that the Box should not be made, but what has happened here makes clear also that my mind would have been changed. That I would indeed make it. That can no longer be so. For though the muddle our young friend here—both of him—has made perhaps will spread no further, and though *perhaps* nothing but good may come of their warning us of these thieves, the risk is too great. My mind now is like a rock. It is not able to be budged. The world never will be ready for the Box, so there must *be* no Box."

I let my breath out in a shaky sigh.

Jacko drew his in in alarm. "You mean we're stuck here for—for good? And that's why there wasn't anything beyond the time window?" He had that pale-around-the-mouth about-to-be-sick look.

The Professor's bushy eyebrows drew together. "This is a problem? I do not see it to be so. You have parents here. You have a home."

Like he said, his mind is as a rock. And about as practical. He pooh-poohed the idea that Mom and Dad might be a shade flustered at having Mutt turn up with two new brothers out of the blue.

"Pah! If they have eyes in their heads they can see you are of the same blood. Surely they will not turn you from the door."

"Maybe not," Mutt put in craftily. "But they'd sure ask lots of questions. And it's wrong to tell lies, especially to your parents. So we'd have to tell them about the Box, and—"

"And Dad can't keep a secret for more than half an hour," Jacko finished eagerly. "Once I told him what I bought my brother for his birthday. He crossed his heart he wouldn't tell, but next time he wrote a letter to Phil, he forgot and blabbed it right out."

Mutt gave him a funny look. "You mean the time I bought Phil the neat air spray for dusting off his computer keyboard?"

Jacko nodded. "Why?"

Mutt sighed. "I bought it yesterday, and told Dad this morning. Now I'll have to keep reminding him he promised not to tell."

"For Pete's sake," I burst out. "Leave it alone. Don't change anything!" I looked to Professor Poplov to second the warning, but he was off on his own train of thought.

"Hrum. All this I must cogitate upon." He scowled, but then waved his hand. "Be assured, it is a problem for which I shall make a solution. But first we must attend to these idea-pirates. I will look now at this message Woody says he has left on my calendar file."

He led the way through to Lab B, sat down at the terminal, logged on, went pecking through the keys with two fingers, and called up the message Woody had planted.

EUREKA! PROJECT DATA & COMPUTATION COMPLETE. WILL ENTER FINAL CHAPTER ON TERMINAL AT HOME TONIGHT & DO REMOTE PRINTOUT

OF COMPLETE DISSERTATION ON E.E. OFFICE PRINTER. SHOULD FINISH & PICK UP BEFORE MIDNIGHT, GET IT TO YOU TOMORROW A.M.!!

"Hah, yes!" Professor Poplov nodded. "This is good. These thieves surely will know enough of us to know that you live in Baxter Hall. They will not like to risk being suspicious to so many students. And so they will concentrate, I think, on the empty office of the department."

Woody nodded. "A chimpanzee with mittens on could fiddle the lock on that printer-room door."

"So! The thieves may fit onto the printer cable a sensor like this nasty one J. J. has described to us, and think to steal away your work, leaving no footprints to betray them. So far yours is a good plan, yes. But will you truly print out the whole of your work? It is a great risk. These thieves transmit by radio to their own computer or printer what they steal. What if the police should not discover who receives at the other end what is transmitted?"

"It's all right, sir," Woody assured him. "I did think of that. There are one or two pages I won't print at all, but there won't be any gap in the page numbers. For the rest, if I change the data and calculations here and there, they can't use my results. It will take them two or three days to find that out."

"Splendid!" Professor Poplov rubbed his hands together. "If Captain Timmons is at home, I shall have arranged all with the police within the hour. Then we will meet at six—excepting for Woody, who must be at work at his terminal in Baxter Hall. I have at six-thirty an engagement, an important dinner at the home of my good friends the Dilleys."

"Me too," Mutt piped up. "It's Mo's birthday."

I winced. Mo the Meddler again. I'd completely forgotten that April twelfth was her birthday as well as Polly's.

Jacko didn't seem surprised, though. "That makes it easy," he said happily. "You can tell Mutt what's up, and he can tell us as soon as he gets home."

The Professor looked blank. "How so? Ah, yes! Because you live only two doors down the street from the Dilleys. Such a curious universe we live in! It is difficult to remember that you two and Mutt are one and the same."

One, maybe, but for sure not the same.

"I don't like any of this," I grumbled.

"Pah! Why should you not?" Professor Poplov pooh-poohed. "What could be better? If I am watched, I shall be doing only what has been planned for weeks. But—Mutt?—Mutt and I shall arrive early. We shall have our little talk, and after dinner he shall tell you what I have arranged."

"And where will Jacko and I be?" I asked sourly. " 'Our' room at home, I suppose."

"Sure. Why not?" Mutt offered eagerly. "And if Mom's at home when we get there, I can unfasten the window and you guys can climb in up the Armbrusters' tree."

Jacko didn't much care for the idea of being parked out of the way like that, chewing at his fingernails.

"I tell you what," he said. "Why not all of us head for the Owl's Nest at six? Then the Professor can clue all of us in at once. J. J. and I can sneak down the alley and whip in without anybody laying an eye on us."

Clearly Mutt was a bad influence. Already Jacko was beginning to sound like him. O.K., so maybe he'd sounded like a stuffed turnip before—I'll admit it—and maybe I had too, but there is such a thing as going too far.

"What is this Owl's Nest?" the Professor growled.

"You know," Mutt prompted. "The house up in the Dilleys' oak tree, out back."

"Ah, yes. The tree house." Professor Poplov looked doubtful.

I didn't like it either. Three guesses who lives in between us and the Dilleys. Righty-ho. The Armbrusters. And I didn't like one little bit the idea of running into—of even *seeing* ten-year-old Polly again. I couldn't have said why. I used to have fun going through the Armbrusters' photo albums with Polly, and seeing her growing up from frilly baby panties to sunsuits, and then frizzy ballet skirts, flower-fairy Halloween outfits, majorette uniforms, and all that stuff. But seeing the actual *her* at age ten again? No, thanks. That glimpse I had at the science fair was just plain creepy. What I wanted was—yes, I really *did*—I wanted to get back to my Polly. The real Polly.

"Oh, the Owl's Nest is strong enough," Jacko assured

the Professor earnestly. "And the ladder's extra strong too. Mo's brother George and my—our brother Phil built it, but Dad showed them how. And Mo's father—"

"I know, I know this," the Profesor snapped. "He takes his books there to read when the house will not be quiet. Very well. The tree house is private, and that is very good. At six o'clock, then."

I think he didn't like the idea any more than I did. If Jacko hadn't made such a point about how strong the Owl's Nest was, he'd have said no. Maybe Jacko didn't know it, but he sure pressed the right button. Suggest to the Professor that he, Nicholas Poplov, was too fat for whatever it was, and he was sure to do it anyway. That's why he took up riding a bike. And how once he ended up hang-gliding off Heavenly Point smack into the surf on Hanna's Beach.

It was four-thirty or so when I climbed out onto the old, familiar maple-tree limb and followed Jacko in through my own bedroom window. It's an O.K. trick when you're still not five feet tall, but fairly hairy when you're six-foot-one, skinny or no. The further out on the limb and the nearer to the window I got, the more the limb sagged. I guess I was in pretty crummy shape, gym workouts or no, because as soon as I caught hold of the window sill, my feet slipped off the limb. I went *splat!* against the house and just hung there. I'd always been lousy at chin-ups, but this was ridiculous. As I puffed and panted to haul myself over the sill I decided that when I got *home*-home, I was going to get Phil's old rowing machine and weights down from the attic and start working out every morning.

The eighty minutes from four-thirty to ten till six felt more like three hours. Me, myself and I, we didn't talk much, (a) because all Mutt could think to say was would this or that happen in the future, and every time Jacko looked like answering, I jumped on both of them. And (b) after all, who has all that much to say to himself? I sure didn't.

So Jacko went snooping around the room, picking up things like my first and favorite soccer shirt, the light sword, and the beat-up old model of the spaceship USS *Enterprise*—junk I got rid of when I was in high school. I felt a twinge or two when I saw the stuff, especially my old H.O. trains set out on their track table. And Waldo, my one-eyed teddy bear. I sent Waldo to the Goodwill with the trains and a lot of other kiddy litter. I think it was right after my first Saturday afternoon movie with Polly. College men didn't need teddy bears. Anyhow, there Waldo was, with his old shy smirk, and I couldn't look him in the eye. Instead, I picked up a library book—*Black Holes*—from the desk, and plopped myself down in the bean-bag chair. Jacko and Mutt set up the chess board and played until Mom called up to say Mutt had to take a shower before he got dressed to go over to Mo's house.

I almost yelled O.K. back right along with Mutt.

Right then, I couldn't have crashed any lower if somebody had cut the elevator cable on me in a skyscraper with umpteen subbasements. It was awful. There was my own Mom downstairs and Dad out in the garage workshop as usual on a Saturday afternoon, and I couldn't go down and tell them it was *me* here. It had to be almost as bad as being dead and coming back as a ghost nobody could see.

I wasn't about to go back out through the window if I didn't have to, so at ten to six Mutt went out into the hall to see whether the coast was clear. Mom and Dad were going to the Dilleys' too. It seems Professor Dilley had proposed making the party a double celebration for Mo's birthday and Mutt's science fair award—which wasn't the way I remembered it, but from here on in, what would be? I wondered if maybe that was Mo's idea. Anyhow, Dad was in the shower by then, and Mom (my mom the culture vulture) in the bedroom singing one of the Susanna bits from the opera *The Marriage of Figaro* while she got dressed. Mutt waited at the top of the stairs until Jacko and I had tiptoed down and were safely out of sight in the kitchen before he yelled, "I'm going, Mom!"

She stuck her head out to look him over. "O.K. You look very nice, honey. Tell Mo's mom we'll be along in half an hour or so."

Mutt went out the front door, and Jacko and I scuttled out the back and into the alley. The fences along our alley are high, so I didn't have to worry about catching an accidental glimmer of Polly. We nipped in through the Dilleys' back gate and, even though the oak trees were screened from the house by hydrangea bushes and a big, fat fig tree, we zipped up the ladder as fast as we could.

It was ages since I'd even thought about George Dilley and Phil's tree house. Maybe a tree house wasn't just dumb kid stuff after all. At least not your ordinary dumb kid stuff. This one has four rooms—two in the middle oak tree and one each in the other two. The whole thing is on different levels, each room up or down a step or two. There are windows and peepholes, a doorway with a half-door and an old-fashioned latch, and a roof that looks as if it might really keep out rain. The main room —at the end—is about as big as our bathroom at home, and the floor space in each of the others is about the size of a small sleeping bag when it's spread out. But what do you expect from scrap wood from the Bay Dump and a bag full of nails? I sat down on the floor next to one of the spy holes, feeling—I guess you could say—almost jealous.

After about five minutes, Mutt and Professor Poplov appeared on the Dilleys' back porch.

With Mo.

I stuck my head out the door when they reached the foot of the ladder.

"What's she doing here?"

Mo stood below with her hands on her hips—in a dress for a change, with a yellow bow in her hair, a camera draped on its strap around her neck and, of all things, a black eye. She gave me a blackish green-eyed glare.

"It's my tree house. George gave it to me."

Jacko laughed. "Who gave you the black eye?"

Mo's cheeks reddened. "Who else? Polly Armbruster. I won a bet and she wouldn't pay me my Mars Bar. So I called her—a name, and she bopped me."

"You made that up, Maureen Dilley," I accused. "Polly wouldn't know how to bop a—a fly."

"That just shows how much you know. Why do you s'pose all the girls call her Polly Arm-buster?"

I must say, Jacko was a disappointment. Not only didn't he seem bothered, he just grinned and asked, "What did you call her to get the black eye?"

Mo gave a sniff. "None of your business."

"Come, come!" Professor Poplov waved Mutt toward the ladder. "Up, up! Maureen too. I shall come last. And you, J. J., need not worry about Maureen. We talk now only of these pirates, and her silence is to be trusted. She has crossed her heart and hoped to die. As she is a woman of honor, that is sufficient." His eyebrows drew together in a scowl. "Is it not?"

Put that way, it had to be.

Mo smirked.

When the Professor's turn came at the ladder it was hard to know whether to offer him a hand or look the other way. We all decided it was safer to look the other way. Mutt and Jacko and I took the side window, and Mo peered into her camera case. Once we heard the Professor's "Phew!" (and the floor creaking), Jacko and Mutt and I turned around again.

Just as Mo's camera flash went off.

"Isn't it neat? See, it gives you instant pictures. It's my birthday present from Uncle Nick." I guess I still wasn't looking too happy, because she scowled right back. "What's biting you?"

"Not a thing. Nothing." If she knew the Professor well enough to call him Uncle Nick, I might as well bite my tongue. We were stuck with her.

Mutt held the Polaroid snapshot for Mo while it darkened and dried. When it had, Jacko took one look and made a face. He passed it on to me.

In it, three of the same startled looks, three heads at the same tilt, with the same hairlines and identical scars on the foreheads, stared out at me. We looked like a top-quality trick photo of a small, regular, and large economy size of the same person. Funny thing, ha ha. I couldn't take my eyes off it.

While I stared, Professor Poplov—who had seated himself in Professor Dilley's beat-up old armchair and managed to catch his breath—began to outline the plan for mousetrapping the thieves. The rest of us sat down on the floor, and while Mo was too busy listening to notice, I slid the photo into my blazer pocket. The thing was too weird and too risky to have floating around.

"Captain Timmons has enlisted the help of the city police," the Professor told us. "When dark falls, the officers will be hiding themselves in the Electrical Engineering building, close to the small office where is the printer. They will hide also in vans of the university grounds and maintenance service to be parked behind the machine shop and the maintenance yard."

Mutt hunched up his shoulders in excitement. I was impressed myself.

"How'd you fix all that so quick?" Jacko asked admiringly.

"Quick*ly*," I muttered. He only shrugged.

Professor Poplov laid a finger aside his nose. "Ah, I have impressed the good captain—who understands nothing of such things, and so asks no embarrassing questions—that millions of dollars in research are at stake. As in truth they are."

"But what about Galaxitronics?" I burst out. "What if that's where their receiver is?"

Leaves rustled outside the window behind me, stirred by the evening breeze.

"Hah!" Professor Poplov held up a pudgy forefinger. "I did not breathe a whisper of Galaxitronics. No! They are too rich. A company so rich as they may have friends with large ears. So, no. Instead, I have hinted only that this receiver may be somewhere in the industrial park up on Humboldt Hill. And so it is arranged that at both gates to the park the police will at half an hour before midnight make of their cars a roadblock, so that all who leave must stop and identify themselves. For you see, once our pirates have placed their sensors on the printer cable, a crime is afoot. If a car is stopped and the driver will not allow the police to search, my good friend Judge Marcus, who waits by his telephone for the captain's call, can issue a search warrant. Then the officers may look for a printout of Woody's project. Or perhaps tapes or disks."

For all of Professor Poplov's absentmindedness and helplessness in practical, everyday matters like not burning the bottoms out of teakettles, once he does manage to get his act together, it really is together.

Jacko crowed. "I bet you five dollars it *is* somebody at Galaxitronics. It has to be."

That's when the rustle of leaves sounded again, but this time there was a noise with it—a sort of muffled squeak—that wasn't made by any evening breeze. I moved to look out the end window, and had to choke back a muffled squeak myself.

Jacko saw too. "Oh, no!" he croaked.

Who wouldn't croak? There, fifteen or so feet away, on the other side of the high garden fence, in the nearest of the Armbruster oak trees, hung little Apollonia Anne Armbruster. Literally. By her hair, one arm, one leg, and the bow to the sash of her pink party dress.

Four of us stood and gaped, but Mo, quick as a lizard, got her revenge for the black eye. There was a flash of light, and then, in a few seconds, another and another.

"You quit that, Maureen Dilley!" Polly shrilled in a purple rage. "You stop that and you help me down. I'll tell if you don't. My Uncle Harry works for Galaxitronics, and I'll tell him every word and he'll tell *every*body."

17

It was no small deal getting Polly down. Getting her to shut up was impossible. Jacko and I climbed over the fence and into the tree, and I had to hold her up by the ankles so she couldn't drop any further while Jacko worked at undoing the snaggle of long, blond hair. The whole time, she was yelping, or yelling, "Ow! *Ow!*" or shrilling, "I'll tell. I will. I'll tell!" Once Jacko got her hair untangled, I hauled her up so he could untie the sash. When we had her loose, I had to sling her over my shoulder Tarzan-fashion so I could climb back down.

All that hassle, and all the thanks I got was "Put me *down,* you—you—you—" and her pounding me on the back with her fists. My head was in a whirl. My world, as they say in the old cliché, was crumbling around me. All over again. *This is Apollonia? Sweet-voiced, soft-eyed, tender-hearted Apollonia Armbruster?* Maybe she was in shock. She *had* almost had a nasty fall. Shock. That had to be it.

As soon as I was far enough down the tree, I hauled her off my shoulder and lowered her by one wrist to Professor Poplov below.

Mo was still snapping away happily with a wide, gleeful grin as fast as the instant photographs came whirring out: Polly over my shoulder with her hair hanging down over her face, Polly dangling, Polly glaring. When the Professor set her down on her own two feet, she was so boiling mad you could almost see the steam coming out of her ears. I thought for a minute she was going to go for Mo and the camera, but she took a deep breath and didn't. I guess it was a question of first things first. She dusted off her crumpled dress, retied the sash, brushed back her long, silky hair, tangles and all, and put on a wide smile that showed her eyeteeth. What with the steam still rising, so to speak, and her eyes glaring, if only she'd had long, black hair instead of blond, she'd have made a first-class Draculette.

"So very interesting," she said sweetly, batting her eyes at the Professor and then me. "All that stuff I heard. Absolutely fascinating."

Funny thing. Did I say "long, blond hair"? Well, maybe her hair wasn't black, but it wasn't exactly blond either. At least not the blond I remembered. It was more—well, very light brown. O.K., so lots of girls color their hair. No big deal. But those two long eyeteeth . . . ? Maybe she got them fixed. I couldn't be sure. Maybe they only showed when she grinned. When I stopped to think about it, I wondered if I'd ever seen my own Polly with a grin on her face. Sweet smiles, yes. Giggles. No grins.

"In fact," Polly announced, lifting her nose in the air, "I am going into the house this very minute before my party starts and tell my Uncle Harry all about how you were talking about burgling and Galaxitronics and eleven-thirty and getaway cars."

She turned with a twirl of skirt and swirl of sash to

sweep away, but then narrowed her eyes and twirled back. "And if anybody tries to stop me I'll yell bloody murder. My Daddy and Uncle Harry are in the playroom setting up the movie projector, and they'll hear. I'll tell them you *made* me fall. We're going to see *Freaky Friday* at my party," she added smugly, going into a final twirl and stalking away.

Mutt looked at Jacko. Jacko looked at me. I looked to the Professor. But even he was buffaloed.

Not Mo.

"I wonder . . ." She held up a photograph to look at it consideringly, and said in a loud voice, "I wonder how much it costs to get copies made. I bet you I could sell twenty or thirty. More, maybe. *Every*body in Mrs. Tolley's fifth grade would buy one for sure. And a whole bunch of girls in third and fourth grade, I bet."

Polly hesitated, then slowed. But she still kept going, out from under the trees and onto the lawn.

"This one's even better," Mo announced. She riffled through her handful of photos and passed one to Mutt.

Mutt took one look and cracked up in giggles.

Polly stopped, but she didn't turn back. Her fists were clenched. Even from behind her back you could feel she had her jaw stuck out and her eyes squinted up.

"Or this one."

Mo handed one to Jacko. He gave a loud snort, then smothered the rest of the laugh behind his hand. I couldn't see the photo that set him off. I wasn't sure I wanted to.

Polly turned and glared.

"Actually—" Mo tilted her head and looked thoughtful. "I think this one's best of all. Don't you, Uncle Nick?"

Professor Poplov, who had been watching Mo with a mixture of puzzlement and admiration, took the photo gingerly. But then his eyes widened and he threw his head back in a great guffaw. Old Saint Nick himself couldn't have let out a heartier "Ho-ho-ho!" His shoulders heaved as he struggled to stop, and as his face got redder, Polly's got whiter.

The temptation was too much. I grabbed the photo and looked.

Let me tell you, a window dummy would have laughed. There was old Polly, hanging nearly upside down in the oak tree, looking like a pink pretzel. Her hair looked like a mop somebody'd stuck in an electric socket. Her eyes glared, and her mouth was so wide open you could see down past her tonsils.

I guess you could say that was the moment my heart broke. Cracked right in two.

The funny thing was . . . here I'd been feeling miserable for all this time about my Apollonia's dating Max the Shark. Then my heart breaks and all I can feel is—is like I'd just dropped a seventy-five-pound backpack after a thirty-mile hike.

I couldn't figure it.

As for Polly, all she did was tighten her mouth up into a mean, straight line and hold out her hand.

Mo took the photograph away from me and held it up, just out of reach.

"Promise you won't tell what you heard? Not to anybody? Not till tomorrow?"

"I guess." Polly sulked.

"Guess is not good enough," Professor Poplov rumbled. "But if you give your word of promise, and keep it, I promise to you that Maureen shall give to you every one of these photographs she has taken."

Mo blinked. "*All* of them? But what about the next time she pulls a ratty trick? Can't I keep a couple? Just *one*?"

"All. And I shall take charge of them in the meantime," the Professor said firmly. "It is agreed?"

It was agreed, but what did I care? Wasn't everything over? Wasn't I stuck for good in my own past? With a broken heart? Or a black and blue one at least? Well, ye-e-es. But this scratchy little voice at the back of my mind twittered, "Heart, my foot!" O.K., so maybe it was my ego that was bruised. That I could patch up. Think of all the future scientific knowledge in my head that nobody else had yet. As for making a living in the meantime, all I had to do was invent a new Hovertoy, say a—a Hoverblimp. Then I could pay my own room and board and fees at the university, and get back to work on one of my own projects. There would be the little problem of no high-school records, but surely Professor Poplov could wangle me into the university *some*how. He'd have to. Period. And of course he'd make me a research assistant right off. After all, when you got right down to it, most of this mess was his fault. Or would be. Would have been going to be? Whatever.

Anyhow, it wasn't until we were back in the Poplov Labs building—in the dark, up on one of the iron catwalks that had ringed the old original Galaxitron back in its Brain Bin days—that I brought the subject up. We were up there because the police had phoned in the middle of Mo's birthday dinner to report to the Professor that the thieves had turned up at six (in a phone company van this time), parked a block away from the E.E. department, and entered by the front door. Fifteen minutes later they were spotted on the roof, where they were still lurking.

We had a long, itchy wait for the next phone call.

Then, at ten o'clock Woody rang to say he'd finished typing his faked-up last chapter and had entered the command for the remote printer in the E.E. office to start churning out his four hundred-odd pages. Five minutes later, we (Mutt and Mo too, thanks to Professor Poplov's clout with our mystified parents) were on our way to the labs.

From the catwalk that ran parallel to the upper Lab C windows we could see down across the corner of the parking lot to the E.E. building. Some of the security lights had been turned off to help make the burglars feel overconfident. The entrance and some of the office windows were visible, but shrubbery hid the printer-room window. Not that it made much difference, since it was one of those frosted-glass ones. From where we stood you could see a corner of the E.E. roof, too, if you leaned right out over the catwalk rail. Mutt claimed at one point he saw a head pop up above the dark roofline and then down again, but nobody else saw it. I eased a couple of the upper windows open so we could hear anything there was to hear. Which turned out to be nothing. At five minutes to eleven we were still up there, sitting with our legs dangling off the catwalk, wondering what could be holding Woody up. He'd had time to get across campus from Baxter Hall twice and back again.

It was then, when the Professor was going on about what a great researcher Woody was, that I saw my chance and slipped in a casual remark or two about the work I was doing on the holographic imager before our hiccup in time and was itching to get back to.

"Interesting." The Professor pulled at his beard. "Indeed. Yes, hum . . . I had not considered—but come, this is no time to talk of such things. Tonight we are having a venture."

"An *ad*venture," I corrected automatically.

"So it is. So it is," he said vaguely. But he gave me this funny look. People were always doing that. I could never figure out why.

"Hey, look!" Jacko hissed. "Somebody's coming."

A pickup truck nosed in from the street. Under the parking-lot lights it gleamed red.

"It's Woody," I whispered. His pickup wasn't new even then, but it was shiny and looked sharp. When I'd seen it last (so to speak), one fender was held on with wire and insulating tape, and the paint job looked like it had been worked over by half a dozen chimps with ball-peen hammers.

Woody got out, slammed the cab door shut and locked it, and strolled off toward the E.E. building with his hands in his pockets, whistling this birdy music I recognized (thanks to my mom the opera nut) as Mozart's.

Professor Poplov rubbed his hands together and chortled. "Hah! The birdcatcher lures the birds. Very good indeed. So innocent and unsuspecting he sounds!"

Once Woody was out of sight, we crept down the iron steps and hurried out to the front entrance hall, where Captain Timmons had set up what he called his command post (which amounted to a folding chair and a clipboard). He was listening to the soft crackle on his two-way radio.

"The printer is still printing," he announced.

That was no problem—it takes a fair old time to print out four hundred pages—but the captain sounded worried. "Your man Newburger seems to be in pretty high spirits. He waltzed in there with a half-bottle of champagne, and right now it sounds like he's dancing around and singing in some foreign lingo."

"An excellent touch!" Professor Poplov chuckled. "For so would you too dance, my good Timmons, if after twenty-six years you had at last finished school."

"Twenty-six years!" Mo yelped.

"Indeed. Counting kindergarten, twenty-seven. And ten of them he has spent on this project these thieves wish to steal."

Captain Timmons shook his head. "Ten years? Phew! Rather him than me."

"Ah, he is slow because he is thorough. And because

of this he becomes a good scientist. Better than good. Excellent. I, Nicholas Poplov, who should know, say it."

"Glad to—sorry, Professor." Captain Timmons held up a hand and broke off to listen to the soft, crackly voice that suddenly spoke through his transceiver.

"*. . . printer has stopped, and the guys on the roof seem to know it. They must have left a bug down there. Baker says one of them has just moved over to the corner of the roof on your side. He's got to be watching for Newburger to come out.*"

Captain Timmons drew a deep breath. There was next to no light in the hallway from the lamppost outside, but you could tell he had sucked in his gut and was trying to look like he was an old hand at SWAT operations, not just chief of a little five-man force whose idea of a big weekend was having to knock on more than four fraternity-house doors to ask them to keep the party noise down.

"Roger," he snapped into the radio. "We move as soon as they leave the roof. Over and out."

"*Uh—yessir,*" it crackled back.

Two minutes after Woody drove off again in his pickup, Captain Timmons slipped out to supervise, as he put it, "drawing the net tight around the perpetrators." We were left peering out the front door.

"Drawing the net tight" may sound neat and tidy. Dull, even. Well, the net was drawn neatly and tidily tight, all right. But it wasn't exactly dull, because the fish weren't in it. Cops hiding at the far end of the roof tippytoed across and followed the perpetrators (now there's an overstuffed word for you) down the emergency access stair. More cops crept out of cupboards and johns and moved toward the printer room from the offices on either side; and over in the maintenance yard cops charged out of vans and rushed in to cover the building's six exits.

Zero. Zilch. I wish I could have seen Captain Timmons's face when he opened the printer-room door. Not that it wasn't exciting. It just wasn't exciting for the cops. They grumbled about missing all the fun, but the rest of us had almost more of it than we could handle.

What happened was, as soon as Captain Timmons slid out of the Poplov Labs, the Professor, Mo, and the three of me all had our noses up against the windows in the double doors.

"Can anybody see anything?" Mutt complained. "All I see is bushes."

Bushes were about all there was to see. The windows of the printer room some twenty yards away, and the offices on either side, were almost completely hidden behind a thick mass of oleanders.

"But the burglars can't see *out* through them either," Mo whispered.

So? So what? So, I had been a pretty dim bulb all day. Why stop now? I didn't catch on even when I saw her shadowy white sock draw back, and Mutt jump as if he'd just had a sharp kick in the ankle. The next thing the Professor and Jacko and I knew, the doors had opened and were swinging back toward us.

What choice did we have? We had to go after them.

Snatch the little kiddies out of the line of fire and all that. Except, seeing as those two could very likely look after themselves better than we three, your sensible, mature adult would have stayed put. But who's a sensible, mature adult twenty-four hours a day? When it gets too much for you, I say drop the act and settle for being a sensible, mature kid. So we nipped out after them.

That's how come, when the *Police!-Come-out-with-your-hands-in-the-air* ruckus started, we were crouching in the shrubbery, feeling cheated because all we could see was this little pinprick light from a penlight moving around inside. (Did it occur to us that if the casement window had been shut, all we could have seen was a small, blurry glow? No, it did not.) Anyhow, that's when the lights sprang on in the side offices. A split second later a big, dark something—well, slightly big—came sailing out to crash through the oleanders and bowl Professor Poplov over backward. He went down with a loud *Oof!* just as a second dark figure, surprised by the *Oof*, hesitated in midleap and ended up stuck in mid-shrub.

"I got him! I got him!" Mutt yelled, grabbing at a flailing foot.

"Me too!" Mo screeched, dragged off her feet as she clung to the other foot.

Jacko jumped up to get an arm around the guy's neck, yelling, "Help the Professor!" at me. Next thing I knew, I was hauling this strong, sharp-elbowed, shin-kicking *female* off poor Professor Poplov. I mean to tell you, I almost got flattened. By the time the cops got their act together and came galumphing around the corner to slap the handcuffs on the two of them, Professor Poplov had caught his breath, the security light had been switched on, and I was having a hard time not moaning with the pain. Woody came galloping back just in time to miss out on taking his share of the lumps.

But there they were. Our pirates. At last. And all got up in neat black outfits with black gloves and black ski masks like they'd been watching too many cookie-cutter TV crime shows. Captain Timmons seemed to think he was acting in one himself, the way he went all stern-faced, stalked up, and whipped their ski masks off with a dramatic sweep of his arm.

Well!

The Professor looked more puzzled than surprised, but you could have knocked me over with the proverbial wing thing.

The female was Dr. Mona Crawford, the blond, brainy Galaxitronics research—some research—director we had seen at the science fair.

And the other one? *I* was surprised, even if Jacko wasn't.

You guessed it.

Max Sharp.

18

Professor Poplov gave a snort. "By all that's edible! Dr. Crawford! *You?* And this young man—Sharp, isn't it? The other waveform recorder project at the science fair? I do not understand. How can such persons, of such abilities, be parties to—to *this*?" He held out the captured impulse sensor between thumb and forefinger as if it was a rotten fish.

Max and the Galaxitronics research director ignored him. They stood defiantly, eyes on the treetops, mouths tight, and both calmly brushed locks of flyaway blond hair back to their usual smoothness.

Mutt whispered to Mo. Mo whispered back.

"*We* think she's his mother," Mutt announced.

The Professor's eyes narrowed. The Captain's widened. Dr. Mona Crawford forgot her defiance and looked indignant. But she kept her mouth shut.

Professor Poplov held up a hand. "No, I think not. But there is something. Definitely something . . ." He peered at her intently, as if she were a baffling mathematical problem. "Sharp," he muttered. "Sharp. *Sharples!*" He laid his finger alongside his nose. "Hah! Yes. Many years ago—in New Jersey it was—I knew a very young lady of the name Nikki Sharples, the little daughter of a student of mine. Now, if Nikki was short not for Nicole, but for Monica, *presto!* here is Mona, which also can be short for Monica. And her baby brother, I would guess. But why? I do not understand this."

Neither one of them let out a peep. Not, that is, until the officer who was keeping in radio contact with the city police out at the industrial park bellowed out, "Hey, Chief—they think they've got him! Guy in his fifties in a big Mercedes with a Galaxitronics parking sticker. They say he has a box full of stuff on computer paper in the trunk. Name's Sharp."

At that, Dr. Crawford stiffened, and Max wilted like a tulip in a sauna bath.

Once the two younger Sharps (Mona Crawford's I.D. read "Mona Sharp Crawford") were driven off to the police station with their mouths still firmly shut, Professor Poplov told us what he remembered about their dad, who had to be the guy in the big Mercedes. It seems that some twenty-nine or thirty years back, in the dark ages before the silicon chip, when computers were as big as dinosaurs, the Professor was teaching at some university in New Jersey and had this graduate student named Lomax Sharples. Sharples was fresh out of the army and was all hot-eyed about becoming an electronics wizard. Trouble was, he may have been sharp, but he didn't have any of what you'd call—well, *whiz.* Without which, no wizard is worth a wet washrag. Worse, he had this swashbuckling idea that if you concentrate on the big details, the little ones take care of themselves. Which for a scientist is, you might say, a trifle upside down. At that point, Professor Poplov began to wonder how Sharples got through his first four years, so he went into a telephone huddle with the registrar at Sharples's old college. It turned out that Sharples, Lomax J., had forged himself a New Improved transcript of grades with Bs instead of Ds and As instead of Cs. So after he finished hitting the ceiling, the Professor resigned as Sharples's research supervisor. The university ushered Sharples out the nearest door before he could say, "But—"

To hear Sharples tell it, he was a misunderstood genius. "That Russky, Poplov" had torpedoed him out of pure jealousy.

"I! Jealous of such a one as Lomax Sharples!" Professor Poplov threw up his hands. "But of course no one believed him."

Woody shook his head in amazement. "And you think he did all this for revenge? He must have been halfway off his rocker from the start. Must *still* be."

But Professor Poplov was already staring absently off into the darkness. "What? Ah, yes, very likely. But, come: it is late, very late indeed for our two small friends here. I think you, Woody, must drive Mutt and Maureen home. J. J. and Jacko will come with me."

I guessed the two of us would be bunking at the Professor's house until he figured out what to do with us. Anyhow, once Woody and the kids were gone, we followed him over to Bowdoin Street, where his car was parked. Jacko was suddenly stumbling with weariness and yawning like mad, and I caught the yawns from him. (After all, come to think of it, add it all up, and I'd had something like a thirty-four-hour-long day.) But suddenly Professor Poplov stopped smack in the middle of the deserted street and for a good thirty seconds stood glaring at a lamppost on the other side. Then, just as suddenly, he made an about face, and hustled us back toward the lab building, muttering all the way. When we got there, he shoved us in ahead of him, double-locking every door behind us all the way in to Lab C.

Jacko and I stood baffled in the dark.

"Now what?"

"Now we wait," the Professor announced.

"What time it is?" I asked warily. If what was up was what I thought was up . . .

A tiny light flickered on and off as Jacko peered at his digital watch. "Sen—" He cleared his throat. "Seven minutes to twelve."

Twelve o'clock. That second recall I programmed! I couldn't believe it. Professor Poplov was waiting to see whether the Box's time window was going to open up on schedule. In two minutes. And if, by some weird pleat in time it did, then what? Use that window into Nothing to get rid of a couple of uncomfortable complications? Boot us out through it, Destination Unknown? Impossible. For all his furious fits of temper, the Professor Poplov *I* knew couldn't bring himself even to set a mousetrap, let alone—I stared at his bulky shadow silhouetted against the windows lamplit from the street. A hulking, almost threatening shape . . .

O.K., maybe I had been bent out of shape by the

whole long, weird day. Even so, I should have known better. But oh, no. I had to go for the whole blithering idiot bit.

"You—you can't!" I sputtered. "You wouldn't. You *won't*. You won't con *me* into stepping into that—that Black Hole."

Professor Poplov scowled. "What *are* you blathering about?" he growled.

"Come on, J. J.," Jacko snapped, waking up. "Do you *have* to be such an everlasting beanbrain? It's embarrassing."

"Ho, hush!" The Professor, ignoring us both, stiffened, then quivered like a fat, excited bird dog on point. "There! See there? It begins." I could hear his hands rubbing together as he chortled, "Oho—ha!"

Sure enough, there, in the same old spot dead opposite the door, the Box's window was taking form: not a blacker hole in the lab's midnight shadows, but a pale glow that brightened slowly into shadowy afternoon. At the heart of its glow, the center of the future projection-field platform appeared to hang shin-high in midair.

I whirled on the Professor. Talk about U-turns! I could have kissed him. "You changed your mind! You *are* going to build the Box! The recall's working. That has to mean that eight years from now the time loop's going to be completed. Mutt *will* be in the right place at the right time."

"Woody's going to be upset," Jacko suggested. But his voice was squeaky with relief.

And me? Relief was hardly the word. "He'll get over

it," I said with an idiotic grin. "Why'd you change your mind, sir?"

"Why?"

Professor Poplov shook his head regretfully. "Alas, J. J., it is that you know too much to stay here in what you call 'the past.' Too much, not only of what will be done in this laboratory, but in the world beyond. And you will use this knowledge. You mean no harm, but already you have been thinking of developing ideas now which otherwise will one day occur to young Mutt. Woody was right. Let the future come in its own time. But if that is to be so, I *must* build Pandora's Box, and afterward destroy it. I must do so in order that you may leave this here-and-now." He looked at his watch. "Within the next four minutes. So that what you will have done here remains only a—how did you call it?—a hiccup in time."

"But what will you tell Woody? And Mutt?" I stalled wildly. Two-thirds of me wanted to take a running jump for *whatever* lay waiting eight years ahead, but suddenly the other third was dragging its heels. For the first time (a little late, I grant you), it got through to me that the future he wanted me to buzz off to wouldn't be the same one I had left.

". . . and the Box afterward? What will we—"

"Tsk! Talk, talk, talk!" Professor Poplov exploded. "*Go!*"

I wavered.

Jacko didn't. He was gone.

So I took a deep breath and followed.

Mutt's Again

1

That next morning I was in the bathroom brushing my teeth when I looked out the window and saw Professor Poplov's car go past our house and the Armbrusters' and pull up in front of the Dilleys'. I rinsed, hopped out of the bathroom while I was pulling on my jeans, pulled on my Star Wars T-shirt while I hurried down the stairs, and sat down at the breakfast table just long enough to tie my shoelaces. My mom was nowhere in sight, so I glugged down my orange juice, shoved the cereal box in the cupboard, the milk in the refrigerator, my unused bowl in the dish rack, and beat it out the front door.

The Dilleys were sitting around the breakfast table in their bathrobes, listening to Professor Poplov tell about the capture of the research pirates. When Mrs. Dilley saw me at the back door, she motioned for me to come in, pulled up a fifth chair, and served me a plateful from the platter of waffles in the middle of the table.

". . . and," Professor Poplov went on, giving Mo and me this don't-you-dare-say-a-word-about-you-know-what look, "as soon as Woody brought you two home, my other two young friends went home also."

J. J. and Jacko *went home*? I opened my mouth to blurt out "How?" but Professor Poplov waggled his white eyebrows so fiercely that I took a big forkful of waffle instead.

"*And*, after I have seen them go," he said pointedly, "I took myself home and to bed. This morning very early I have gone to the police station and found out what has been learned from the police back in New Jersey, and from young Max, who is too frightened to keep silence any longer. It is this—"

According to Professor Poplov, once Lomax Sharples got kicked out of the university back in New Jersey, he found a job as an electrician and Swore Revenge. After a couple of years he was able to set up as an electrical contractor. A couple more and he had branches in Maryland and Virginia, and a fat contract from the Department of Defense. But well-off or no, he still ground his teeth at the thought of Professor Poplov. And he began to plot.

First off, he bribed a lab assistant and got his hands on the specifications for the Professor's current project, then he mailed them off in a plain brown envelope to this researcher in Rhode Island he knew was working along the same line. The Rhode Island guy decided not to look a gift invention in the mouth, ran up a working model, and applied for a patent. But after that Professor Poplov came up with something else, so where was the satisfaction?

That's when Sharples *really* got going. The Professor moved here to California, so Lomax J. came out to scout around for a business to use for cover, and lucked into Galaxitronics when it was first trying to get off the ground. He changed his name to Sharp, bought a fat share of the company, and moved his family out from the East. Now, all this time he had been feeding his kids Mona and Max on the fairy tale that the Professor had stolen the idea for the PowerJack, the first big Poplov money-spinner, from their dear daddy. And once "Maxwell Sharp, Sr." was settled in, he set out, out of pea-green jealousy, to ruin Poplov Labs by siphoning off any promising research he could get a line on. He kept the whole operation in the family. The spy gear, including the supersensor he used on Woody, came from his Maryland company. Some of the stolen ideas got farmed out to the companies back East. Others Dr. Crawford reworked for Galaxitronics. The Sharples family was on its way to getting filthy, stinking rich.

"Until last night!" Professor Poplov finished triumphantly, rubbing his hands together, and then settling down to work on his own plateful of waffles.

"Well, it must have all been very exciting," Mr. Dilley said. "But what I'd like to hear more about is this impulse sensor you say they used." He hunched over the table. "Tell me, was it—"

So. Back to normal. In the next eight years nothing ever happened to me in any whole *year* two percent as exciting as those twelve hours on April twelfth. Until yesterday, that is. In fact, the J. J.-and-Jacko bit was all so exciting that it wasn't until Mrs. Dilley congratulated me that I remembered I'd won the first prize at the science fair.

Anyhow. To cut the suspense: the Sharpleses were tried and convicted on charges of industrial espionage and packed off to jail. And Professor Poplov *did* build Pandora's Box, with Woody's help. Mine, too, since they didn't set to work on it until well after Woody was made an associate professor two years ago, and after I'd already been working as their Lab C research assistant for a year and a half. They figured that, for security's sake, the later we started on the Box the better. So we built it in under eighteen months, and under deep level security. To keep anybody from guessing we were up to something, we even ordered all the hi-tech high-security gear—electronic locking systems, alarms, window sensors, pressure and heat sensors, motion sensors—in small lots from different suppliers around the country and installed them ourselves. As for the Box's controls, Professor Poplov wrote such a fiendishly complicated master program for its supercomputer that not even Woody or I could understand much of it. I guess that was the idea.

The power supply problem was almost fatal. After the Sharples scandal, Galaxitronics hung on by its eyelashes, but work on their main project, the Galaxitron, slowed to a snail's shuffle. So where were the massive boosts of power the Box needed going to come from? The Professor's new hyped-up, high-energy version of his old PowerJack had increased its input by a quarter, but so what? We still needed those millions of "borrowed" Galaxitron volts. To get them, Professor Poplov ended up selling his patent for the old original PowerJack to the big camping supply company that manufactured it.

With the proceeds he bought a stake in Galaxitronics and a seat on the board of directors. The rest of the board got their act together, and the company started to move again. *And* the Professor talked Mr. Dilley into joining Galaxitronics as research policy director. So the Dilleys didn't move to San Diego like Jacko said they were going to after all.

And nobody ever got a whiff of Pandora's Box.

Yesterday—April twelfth, the Fatal Day—the Box was ready. We weren't sure *we* were. We had run every basic equipment test backward and forward and upside down. But no operations test. No Time-Tinkering Whatsoever Allowed. We agreed on that even though it meant we wouldn't have Idea One about what might happen once we entered the recall command.

We all arrived hours early. Zero Hour wasn't until half past five, but even the Professor got in before eight. Woody, always thinking, came with a jumbo picnic thermos of coffee, a sack of apples, and a big bag of cinnamon rolls. I ate one roll. I turned down a second.

"I think—" I swallowed nervously. "I think maybe one was one too many."

"Pooh, pooh!" The Professor scoffed. "What is it that you believe will happen? Um? All is in readiness. All that can be done has been done. Eh, Woody?"

"What? Oh, yes. Sure." Woody went on nervously shuffling papers from his in tray to his out tray, and then back again. He wasn't in much better shape than I was.

The Professor never noticed. "There, you see," he rumbled. "Nothing to worry about."

Great. Fine. O.K. But in that case why, as the day dragged on and we tried to settle down to more humdrum work, did he have to keep drumming his fingers on his desk, on his knee, on the Box's casing—on whatever—if he wasn't worried? First off, what if our Box was fatally different from Box A? What if *nothing* happened at our end? And what would it mean if nothing did? That J. J. and Jacko had left the past and were floating around in some dark, Star-Trekish limbo? Or, worse, that there never had been a J. J. and Jacko, and that Woody and Professor P. and I were all Class A candidates for the funny farm?

Anyhow, you get the idea what kind of day it was.

At a quarter to five we rolled the Horrible Box out of its vault and lined it up on the Imager's projection-field platform.

At five o'clock we hooked the cable up to the old Galaxitronics outlet.

At 5:10 Woody and I hung over Professor P. as he sat down at the Box's console and switched on the power. The *thrum-hum* built up to a deep whine as the banks of klasers came on-line.

5:12. We synchronized our watches.

At 5:13 Professor Poplov tapped out on the keyboard his auto-recall sequence, then unfolded a limp, dog-eared old scrap of notepaper and entered the recall times J. J. had given him eight years ago.

On the dot at 5:15 he pointed a plump forefinger on the ENTER button, squeezed his eyes shut, and pushed it.

Nothing. Nada. Zil . . .

Zingo!

Incredibly, there it was, exactly as I imagined it would be: a faint shadow in the air, a dim patch where the light grew steadily dimmer and the shadows deeper. It seemed to go on for an hour, but when I looked at my watch only sixty seconds had passed.

Woody and I grinned at each other shakily. The Professor stayed at the console, watching over his shoulder with a scowl. But his forehead glistened with little prickles of sweat and he breathed in quick little puffs. "*Pooh-pooh-pooh-pooh-pooh* . . ."

Two minutes passed. No Jacko. No J. J.

"Something's gone wrong—" I gulped. My stomach rolled over. "I—I've got to go to the john."

"No. Not now." Woody clamped his hand on my arm. "There. Look!"

He was right. Something had moved within the shadow. Next thing I knew, there was this perfectly solid-looking hand groping along the platform beyond the shadow's edge. A moment later Jacko emerged head-first, cautiously, blinking in the sudden light.

"Is it O.K.?" he asked uncertainly. We must have been standing there goggling as if he was Bigfoot or the Abominable Snowman come to tea.

Professor Poplov pulled out a red bandanna handkerchief and mopped his face. "Indeed, indeed," he croaked.

Woody was next to recover. "Come on, Jacko. You'd better step down. You're blocking J. J.'s way."

Jacko moved slowly, kind of like he was wading through molasses. He turned in a daze to peer at the time window. "He kept stalling. I got scared we'd run out of time."

I moaned. "I wish he'd get a move on."

But already I felt better. Our Box worked. And we knew that J. J. *had* followed Jacko through the time window. I straightened my tie and brushed a speck of lint off my new navy blue blazer. And straightened my tie again. Normally you'd never catch me dead in a tie and jacket when I wasn't headed for church or maybe some scientific conference. But even though Woody said it was nuts, I had figured that just to be on the safe side, maybe I ought to rig myself out the way J. J. had looked when we first saw him at the science fair eight years ago. Make things as close as possible to the way they were for him the first time around. Just in case there was something to all that "time loop" jazz. Professor Poplov's comment was, "Pah! Superstition!" but I bought the blazer anyhow. It was so new the pockets were still stitched shut. I picked nervously at the threads.

Jacko was all a-twitch. "Do we have to wait? J. J. doesn't have to be here for you to zap me back—back home, does he?"

"Alas, he does." Professor Poplov sounded more than a shade nervous himself, and answered without taking his eyes from the shadowy time window. "The Box cannot perform two functions at once. But do not fret yourself. The moment the recall is completed, I shall enter the new commands and send you on your way."

Jacko looked about as happy as a cow in quicksand.

Funny . . . Woody said afterward he never noticed it—and the Professor didn't either—but right from the minute Jacko's hand groped into sight on the projection platform, I thought it looked, well, *thin.* So did all of him. Not skinny-thin, but thin like not all there. Like if you squint hard enough you could have seen his bellybutton through his shirt, and the Lab B doorknob through his bellybutton. But maybe I imagined it. Sometimes my imagination gets overheated.

"J. J., where *are* you?" Woody muttered, cracking his knuckles with a sound like popcorn popping.

Professor Poplov pulled at his mustache as if he thought maybe it was the peel-off variety. "I do not understand," he growled. "I do not understand."

Me neither. I was biting my fingernails like mad. I *never* bite my fingernails.

And then, right before our beady eyes, the time window began to fade. And fade.

In ten seconds it was gone.

I'd thought I was more rattled than any of us, but I recovered first. If you can call it recovered. What I did was dash over to Jacko, grab him by the shirt collar, and haul him toward the projection platform.

"*Hey!*—ow!"

"We don't have a nanosecond to lose," I babbled. "Unless I happen to be hallucinating, your translucence is—you're getting more transparent by the minute." As soon as I had him planted on the platform, I dashed around to the Box's controls and pulled back out of Auto

Recall to the Main Menu. The Professor came bustling after me like he was a big she-bear and I'd just laid my paws on her prize cub. For all his size, he can really move when he has a mind to.

"Hang on!" Woody yelped. "What about J. J.?"

"Later. No time." I was already in the middle of tapping out the good old EDWFR file commands that had started this whole flapdoodle by landing J. J. in Jacko's time.

Nothing.

There wasn't even a hiccup in the Box's hum.

I panicked. "Something's wrong. What's wrong? I did it exactly—"

Professor Poplov pushed me aside with a snort. "Exactly. That is the problem. You did it 'exactly.' You forget—" He tapped the INTERRUPT KEY, then ESCAPE, and began typing so fast it was hard to follow the command symbols as they blipped across the screen.

"You forget," he growled, "that though this Box has the capabilities J. J. described to me, the control programs cannot be the same as those of J. J.'s time. Because of the different circumstances of its making and the greater concentration of my mind in designing it, I will surely have taken different routes to the same answers. And I have added secret security protocols I have not revealed even to you and to Woody, my friends."

I was only half listening. My eyes were glued to Jacko and the noonday shimmer that slowly brightened the air around him.

He turned, stepped down, turned back to wave, and was gone.

"But what *about* J. J.?" Woody repeated faintly.

The Professor had already shut the Box down. Opening up the panel behind the little supercomputer's keyboard, he calmly pulled out one of the circuit cards that controlled the Box and began cutting it into snippets with a pair of tin snips.

"I think," he answered, "you must ask Mutt. Ask why he should think he knew the Box's command sequences."

Woody blinked, and turned to stare at me.

I jammed my hands in my blazer pockets. "How should I know? I suppose I just remembered it from what J. J. said. So, I got carried away and forgot none of that had anything to do with this Box. What's so weird about . . ."

And then I remembered.

I fingered a piece of card in my pocket nervously. *J. J. had never told anyone but the Professor anything about the Box.*

The thing was, *I* remembered telling him. It was a little fuzzy around the edges, but I did remember. What's more, I remembered things like how glad I was to see old Mo at the science fair, and how I'd missed her after her folks moved away.

But that first memory belonged to J. J., who *had* told the Professor. And the second was either his or Jacko's, because the Dilleys *hadn't* moved away. And there were more memories where those came from.

"Oh, wow," I said (I always seem to come up with these profound comments at times of stress). I fished the card out of my pocket and looked at it absent-mindedly.

It was the picture Mo had snapped of Eeny, Meeny, and Miney. The one I'd seen J. J. slip into his pocket up in the Owl's Nest tree house.

"Oh, wow," was right.

2

I suppose you could say I've got myself together at last. And all those memories I didn't have before? Remembering them feels more like remembering an old movie than anything else. Clear, but not exactly—real. *I'm* the real me. Me, myself *and* I. When you come right down to it, my having different memories of the same stretch of time is sort of like your imagining what life would have been like if you'd—well, gone out for playing the trombone instead of learning how to use a bandsaw. Like seeing that if you'd done (a) or (b) instead of (c) you'd have ended up at (g) or (o) instead of (x). It's *choices* that make the future. Well, accidents too, but you know what I mean. Look at where I'd be if Jacko had made it to Polly's fourteenth-birthday party!

As for the way things *did* turn out, Professor Poplov really meant it about scrapping Pandora's Box. He already has another project in mind for the supercomputer and the klasers, so all there is to do is strip the rest of it for parts. I'll be glad when it's over and done with.

The Sharples family? After the three of them got out of jail they up and, to everybody's relief, disappeared. Australia, look out! is my advice. As for Polly, she's as foxy as ever. In both senses of the word. I saw her at Christmas when she came home from this college she goes to in Colorado—in a Maserati complete with ski rack, skis, and the guy who owned the car. And good old Woody? Well, once he was officially Dr. Woodrow Newburger and decided to teach at the university instead of going to work for Galaxitronics or Macro Research at twice or thrice the money, guess what? Doris deserted. Woody was so crushed he wandered around in a daze for days, and one afternoon wandered across Thompson Boulevard downtown without waiting for a green light. Talk about dumb luck: (a) it was a VW Bug that got him, and not some big trailer rig, (b) all it broke was one leg and a couple of ribs, and (c) the doctor at the medical center who taped him back together again was funny, pretty, and named Janice. They've been married for over seven years, and they have this little kid they named Nicole so they could call her Nicky, after Professor Poplov.

What else? Oh, yeah. You remember that black eye Polly gave Mo all that time ago? It turned out the Mars Bar bet Polly backed out of was over which waveform recorder project the judges would like better at the science fair. Max's *looked* so sharp that Polly said I never had a chance. When I won and she wouldn't pay up, Mo called her a stinking pink pig.

And Mo? Like I said, Professor Poplov talked her dad into joining Galaxitronics as research policy director, so the Dilleys never did move to San Diego. After I started at the university, I still used to see her around, but up through yesterday I'd been so eyebrow-deep in work on the Box that I hadn't really registered that she wasn't still wearing Sylvester the Cat T-shirts and Band-Aids. If I had, I might have stopped to take some serious thought on the subject before now. I always liked her when I was a little kid because she was funny and had a great right hook, but *now* . . .

Would you believe it? She skipped two grades in junior high, and now she's a freshman in the electrical engineering department. Ours. Here. Electrical engineering! Can you beat that?

And you know, her eyes aren't just green. They've got these little flecks of gold in them.

She's—

Well. Let's just say that when it came to girls, J. J. sure had his wires crossed.

So.

So Mo and I are going to the movies tonight.